Attention Span

and other stories

Attention Span

and other stories

Pauline Wiles

Author's Note

Although these stories take place in different countries,
this book uses British spelling and grammar conventions.

Acknowledgements

This story collection came together over several years and I was cheered by encouragement from many quarters.

I'd especially like to thank Julie Valerie, Janell Beals at *House of Fifty* magazine, and the team at *Toasted Cheese Literary Journal*.

Reader Connie T. gets a special mention for providing the inspiration behind *The List Maker*, as does the nameless bus driver on the Stonehaven – Auchenblae route in May 1983. His kindness stayed with me for thirty years, then found creative expression in *Daffodils*.

I'm grateful to proofreader Wendy Janes for her attention to detail and insightful comments. Any remaining blunders in the text are mine.

And as usual, my husband Darius Wiles provided not only cover design, formatting help and technical expertise, but priceless moral support too.

Attention Span

and other stories

Daffodils

The press never got tired of hearing this story.

Even though Izzy was bored of telling it, magazines and newspapers loved to hear about her first day of paid work and the profound effect it had on the scraggy girl who would grow up to be voted Scotland's leading businesswoman, three years in a row.

'You picked daffodils?' said the journalist, a sandy-haired young man with a striking russet beard. 'At the tender age of ten?'

'Yes,' said Izzy politely, although to herself she thought, *not so tender, really*.

Harvesting daffodils had been one of the few paying options available to teenagers living in the Grampian villages. In the autumn, it was potatoes – tattie picking – wetter, muddier, colder. By September, the weather climate in the mountains around Aberdeen could already be harsh.

But in spring, plucking yellow buds from the green hillsides sounded almost romantic. Izzy had to beg her mother to let her gobble down some toast and sprint to the war memorial in the middle of the village, where the minibus was due to pick workers up at five. Mum was exhausted. She had been at the laundry since six, stooped over the endless sheets from nearby hotels and overalls from the meat factory.

'Go if you must,' she'd said to Izzy. 'Just get away out o' mae hair.'

She knew her mother was dying for a cigarette, but too stubborn to smoke one in front of her only daughter. Izzy tugged on her wellington boots, now a size too small, and half ran, half hobbled to the pickup point. The bus, which turned out to be a ramshackle van, was just pulling away, but stopped when Izzy hollered and waved frantically, desperate not to miss her first chance to earn a wage.

'But when you got there, you weren't impressed?' The journalist seemed content to rehash an old story.

Izzy shook her head. 'Ten daffs made a bunch. A bunch was worth two pence.'

She paused, as she always did here, for the reporter to work out how bad that wage was.

'This was the early eighties, of course, it went a wee bit further then,' she clarified.

'Still, a hard way to make a living,' said the reporter rhetorically.

Izzy didn't bother to agree with him. If he couldn't even phrase a question...

She glanced at the clock on the wall behind him. They were in her office, a comfortable space with springy carpet and sage green walls, which Izzy found both calming and encouraging. A potted plant sat on the coffee table between her and the reporter: even today, she couldn't bear to buy cut flowers, always wondering what pitiful wage had been paid for their harvest.

'So you quit,' said the reporter, clearly knowing the answer already. Izzy's story had been widely shared.

'Well, I didn't give notice, if that's what you mean. I just queued up to get paid for the bunches I'd picked, then walked away.'

'How many bunches?'

'Twenty.' Two hundred daffodils. Izzy had been one of the youngest there, kids much older than her bent over the rows of tightly budded blooms. All of them counted carefully, some muttering aloud, before applying the rubber bands with sap-soaked fingers.

'So, your first pay packet was forty pence?'

'Yes,' said Izzy.

'And then what? You could nae get home again? The minibus wasn't leaving until eight?'

'That's right. I worked out by half past six I was being exploited.'

'And you started walking? Towards home?'

Really, this interview was beyond the pale. He hadn't asked her anything original. The next question was bound to be –

'And how far was it?'

'About fifteen miles,' Izzy replied, suppressing a yawn. Generally, she didn't mind being interviewed, although she'd much rather discuss the company's future plans than this legend. 'But it didn't matter, because I hadn't gone far when the bus came.'

'The bus!' The young reporter echoed her words as if she'd said *winged chariot*. 'And it stopped for you?'

Izzy explained that back then, on the country roads, they didn't have bus stops. You flagged the bus down and hopped aboard. She decided to propel the story onwards. She had to pick up milk on the way home, wanted to stop and see Frazer, too.

'So I asked, how much is it, and the driver asked, how much have you got?'

'How much had you got?'

Clearly, the journalist hadn't been listening, unless he was foolish enough to think Izzy got pocket money in those days. 'Forty pence,' said Izzy. 'Obviously.'

'And?'

The driver, whose name badge read F. Paterson, had cocked his head on one side while he considered. Ten-year-old Izzy had stared fixedly at him, waiting for the verdict, hoping desperately for a fare she could afford.

'Then he said, "Well, let's call it fifteen."'

'He didn't take all your wages?'

'No,' said Izzy patiently. They'd established that, after all.

'You think the real fare was more?'

'I'm sure it was,' said Izzy.

'And that's why, years later, when the driver tracked you down, you took him in?'

Maybe this reporter was cut out for the job after all. He certainly had the ability to exaggerate.

'I didn't take him in. I just helped a little.'

It had made the newspaper. Izzy Robertson, newly voted 2010's Scottish Businesswoman of the Year, told the story of her first day's employment to the *Press and Journal*. The bus driver, by then homeless and in failing health, had come forward to claim his fifteen minutes of fame.

Acting anonymously through her solicitor, Izzy had arranged a place for him at an old people's home near Hazlehead Park. The staff who'd helped him unpack a single suitcase reported he had just forty pence in his pocket at the time.

'Remarkable,' said the reporter. 'That you remembered him.' He gestured around Izzy's expansive office with its view of the River Dee, as though this was an excuse to forget her beginnings.

'Not at all. It was a memorable day in my career.'

Swearing never to work for such meagre wages again, Izzy had taken her twenty-five pence profit and turned it into a pound by buying cheap chocolate bars at the village shop and selling them for a bit more at school. Then she'd done it again, and again, until her teachers declared the little business inappropriate and drove it underground.

Izzy crossed her fingers behind her back, still heedful of her mother's abhorrence of lying. 'Mr Murray, it was a pleasure talking to you but I have another meeting.' She slid a promotional brochure across the table to him. 'There's a press pack here, I think it contains all the background information you'll need to flesh out your article.'

Having shown him out, Izzy consoled herself that the soap opera on BBC2 at eight o'clock that night could be considered a meeting. Quickly, she tidied her desk, jotted down three key things to achieve tomorrow, and turned off the lights. Her assistant was long gone, hopefully home with her kids, and with enough energy that she wasn't sending them out daffodil picking to get some peace and quiet.

~ ~ ~

Izzy drove halfway home before stopping at a corner shop for milk, then pulled into the car park of Hamilton House. The railings were missing from the front wall, as many were in Aberdeen, a scar from the war years. But a row of blue hydrangeas made a cheerful effort at order and softened the severe granite walls of the home. The bushes had grown in the four years that Izzy had been coming here, surprised to find she liked the whist drives, tea parties, and Christmas lunches. The old people cackled with delight at the terrible jokes in their crackers, and made valiant efforts to chew corn on the cob with false teeth. She hadn't expected to find a family here, hadn't realised how lonely her single existence had become until she found herself attending singalongs and making Easter cards with the rest of them. But there was something soothing and companionable about sketching eggs and bunnies and, yes, daffodils.

She found him in the smaller of the lounges, playing patience as usual.

'Uncle Fraze,' she said, waiting to interrupt until he tutted and gathered in the cards from a failed attempt.

'Well, young Izzy,' he said, as he always did, oblivious that Izzy was now past forty. 'How's my high-powered lass? Tired of doing deals yet?'

'Not yet.'

After the daffodils and the chocolate selling, Izzy learned to type, and by sixteen was an assistant at a small firm of solicitors. By twenty, she was at a bigger firm, and noticed how long the senior staff spent shredding documents each day. At age twenty-five, Izzy launched a confidential shredding service, followed a few years later by building maintenance and janitorial services. The day before her thirtieth birthday, she purchased her first office building and leased it to a tenant a week later.

Now, Izzy perched on the ottoman beside Frazer's chair and looked around. This wasn't such a bad home, as they went. It smelled of soup as well as disinfectant, and there were enough male residents that the elderly women didn't go after them like prey. Of course there were mishaps, especially among those whose memories were capricious. Things were stolen and later discovered hidden under the pillows of ninety-year-olds who didn't know their own name. And there was a big to-do when a grandmother of twelve helped herself to a jelly baby from her neighbour's tin, not understanding that the container had long ago been re-purposed to hold spare buttons. That incident ended in a trip to casualty.

'I am tired of journalists, though,' said Izzy. 'They just hash over the same old stuff. You know, the daffodils, the bus fare, all that.'

Frazer had been shuffling his cards, but stopped to cough. It was a rasping sound which made Izzy shift on her perch. When his wheezing stopped, he drew in a long, hesitant breath, as if nervous the act of breathing might send his lungs into spasms again. Then he carried on shuffling.

And shuffled.

And shuffled.

'Fraze?' Izzy said finally, when every card must have been randomised at least three times. 'Are you okay?'

Uncle Fraze, who of course wasn't her uncle at all, balanced the pack on his knee and fanned it with one hand, rippling the cards gently so that Izzy could feel the breeze.

'Pick one,' he said, splaying out the pack for her.

Izzy chose quickly. Decisiveness was one trait which had got her where she was today. She looked at the old man, waiting, and when he nodded, she turned it over.

'Six of hearts,' he said. 'I knew you'd pick hearts.'

'Why?'

'I made a deal with myself, that if you picked hearts, I'd tell you something.' Another short wheeze. 'Confess something.'

Izzy waited. Holding her nerve during uncomfortable silences was another of her core skills.

Frazer began to cough again, this time at length.

The two other seniors in the lounge showed no reaction.

Izzy put her hand on his, still waiting.

'It wasn't me,' Frazer said finally, studying the playing card. 'The bus driver, it wasn't me.' He didn't look at her. 'I did drive a bus for a bit,' he added, as if that mitigated his deceit. 'But whoever it was picked you up that night on the road to Auchenblae, it wasn't me.'

'I know,' said Izzy, noticing his untouched medications, laid out beside the cards.

'You knew?' His voice was hoarse. 'And yet you've been paying my room and board for four years?'

'Well, I wasn't certain, but I suspected.'

Now, he wasn't wheezing. He wasn't even breathing, just staring.

'Why? Why would you do that, for an old man... like me?'

Izzy shrugged. She thought of her comfortable home, now owned outright, and her well-padded bank account. She thought of cuddling with her cat, her soap opera on the television. She thought of her mother, in an early grave, the father she never knew, her own dogged determination to claw her way out of circumstances which left her open to exploitation.

'I figured,' she said, 'you might be the same bus driver, and you might not. It didn't really matter.'

She paused, needing time to swallow the lump in her throat and articulate her thoughts.

'I've been there,' she said. 'And I do remember. When you've only got forty pence in your pocket, you don't question the real fare. You don't wait to be thrown off the bus. You just lift your chin, and you meet their gaze. And you take all the help you can get.'

~ ~ ~

Author's note: My first paid work was picking daffodils in Scotland at age eleven. I abandoned this employment after the first few bunches and the bus driver did indeed ask how much money I had, before suggesting a fare for my journey home. But fiction takes over from there, and unlike Izzy, I enjoyed a comfortable, stable childhood.

Captive

It must be nearly time. They're moving sternly among us, brooking no nonsense, checking we're restrained. It's clear they've no tolerance for trouble. Their stares are as sharp as their voices, one transgression after another caught and rectified. The tiniest detail can draw a rebuke. I look down meekly, avoiding eye contact.

Packed in here almost as tightly as cattle, there are rebellious mutterings. But they know our grumbles are hollow. Although there are far fewer of them than us, they have the upper hand: they made absolutely certain we're not armed.

All around me, the human cargo is bleary-eyed, mostly resigned. It's amazing how the shine wore off our optimism. But I suppose fourteen hours and no sleep will do that to folk. We all look rough: the men are unshaven, the women haggard. There's a half-hearted chorus of throat-clearing and yawning.

Personally, I've ceased caring what it will be like when we get there. I just want to arrive, to get this part over with. Anything to end this jolting captivity.

There was food, or tasteless greyish lumps pretending to be food, but barely enough. And I think they knew that with insufficient water, we'd weaken, become drowsy, cause less hassle. They've played this game before. Of that, I have absolutely no doubt.

How did I let myself get talked into this? I fight back the surge of regret. I was conned by the ambiguous promises, the idyllic images. Why else would I have embarked on such craziness?

'Take a good look at the sun,' says the man next to me. 'It's the last you'll see of it, where we're going.'

But I can't actually see it, even now. He's far taller than me, so even with my neck craned, I can't glimpse daylight. And I don't dare stand up. Not with them prowling. Always prowling.

I look at him properly for the first time. Greying beard, spectacles. What did he do to get himself in here? Does he regret it? He's spent most of the journey lolling into me, nowhere to put his chunky legs and wide shoulders. Every time I dozed off, another of his limbs intruded. I know he didn't mean anything by it. There's just no escape from this forced intimacy. My own legs ache; when I move, pins and needles dance up and down my calves. Even if there was somewhere to run to, I'm not sure I could.

'There it goes,' says my neighbour. 'Clouds now. It'll be all clouds, now.'

'You should have thought of that,' chides the dark-haired woman on my other side, 'before you bought your ticket.' Her face is passive, resigned.

I hear a change in the drone of the engine: are we getting close?

Our captors appear tense now, their eyes flit over us in a last minute attempt to make sure nobody's out of line. This is the risky bit, and they know it. If we riot now, no one is safe.

'Still,' I say to the brunette, 'they tell me it's nice. Mild climate, green fields?'

'Oh, it is,' she replies. 'It is. I wouldn't want to live anywhere else.'

There's a whir, a whine, and a clunk from beneath me. As the wheels come down, the announcement from the cockpit follows.

'Ladies and gentlemen, we will shortly be arriving at London Heathrow. Cabin crew, please take your seats for landing.'

My vacation is about to begin.

The List Maker

'That,' I say, collapsing into the hammock and half squishing my sister Madeline, 'was the absolute last straw. From now on I'm going to have a checklist.'

'Didn't your date go well, Al?' Maddie untangles her elbow from mine so she can continue tapping on her phone.

'It was the absolute pits.' I make sure to add sufficient melodrama to my sigh. 'A total waste of a Saturday afternoon.'

As I speak, the Saffron Sweeting church clock chimes four.

Olivia looks up from her low-slung deckchair, where she's polishing a silver coffeepot.

'Where was it you went?'

'He took me bowling. I thought he meant tenpin, you know, the cool kind with loud music and fried food.'

'What kind was it, then?'

'Grass. As in, old people dressed in white and wearing flat caps.'

'Crumbs,' said Olivia. 'I didn't know they still did that.' She wafts the air to discourage a passing bumble bee. It hums off obligingly.

'Indeed they do,' I tell her. 'Although they complain so much about their knees, it has to be a dying sport.'

'And he took you to that? Why?'

I narrow my eyes. 'He's close to his grandfather. Goes every week, apparently.'

'That sounds sweet,' says Maddie, who never got over being the one to discover our own Granddad Dunbar, dead in his chair while we thought he was watching the Atlanta Olympics.

'Quite the opposite. The first time I tried to bowl, the old geezer slapped my bum. So, anyway. I'm making a list.' I pull out my sketchbook, the one I keep near me to capture bits of nature which take my fancy, and flap it to a fresh page. 'I'm going to use it to vet everyone, weed out the time wasters.'

I look up long enough to see Maddie glance at Olivia, but carry on regardless.

'Item one, no bowling fans. Item two, no grandfathers on dates.'

'No wedding rings,' Maddie says helpfully. Then, at the look I give her, she adds, 'It's important!'

'Fine.' I add *no rings* as my third item. Then, writing slowly: 'Smelly. Remember that interesting guy I met online, but it turned out he ran a fish stall on St Ives market? I couldn't live with the pong of haddock.'

'Dirty, too,' offers Maddie. 'I couldn't do dirty.'

We add *yellow teeth, greasy hair,* and *bad breath.*

'Weird ears,' I mutter. I don't like to even *notice* ears. If I'm aware of them, there must be something wrong. Same with toes.

'How will you use your list on a date?' Maddie asks.

'I dunno. Sit there with a clipboard on my knee, I suppose.'

'Won't they think that's strange?'

'I really don't care at this stage.' I'm twenty-nine, the age by which I was convinced I would be married and pushing a pram. Instead, I'm dealing with bowls parties and fish sellers.

'I could code it as an app,' says Maddie, trying to sit up in the hammock but wriggling hopelessly. 'An app would be cool. We'll call it *Rate Your Date.*'

Madeline is just eleven months younger than I am. Frankly, I think there was a mix-up at the hospital. Where I'm cynical, she's enthusiastic. Where I'm a would-be artist, she's a techie genius. She's the one who resets all the electronic clocks in our flat twice a year, and helps Dad with his iPhone and the defrost setting on the microwave. We have the same green eyes, and the same way of sitting with our toes scrunched under our feet when we get nervous, but that's about it.

'Long distance is a pain, too.' Maddie wrinkles her nose, and I bet she's thinking of the guy from Alabama, whom she met in a Javascript class. He was gorgeous and from a wealthy family, but after two trips to his home in leafy Mountain Brook, Maddie said the hassle wasn't worth it.

'Children,' says Olivia suddenly, holding up the coffeepot to examine her reflection. She used to use that word on Maddie and me when we were younger, a disapproving multisyllable sigh, as though the eight-year age gap made her Mary Poppins.

'What?' I'm still thinking about the dangers of distant love. My farthest boyfriend lived in Inverness, but that was still a pain.

'Whether he wants kids,' Olivia clarifies. 'Yes, no, later.'

Being the eldest, Liv is the responsible, diligent one who knows where the candles are when there's a power cut. As a result of this competency, she networked her way into a fantastic job: long-term house-sitting for wealthy people. Sometimes, when they're away, they let her have guests, which is why Maddie and I are swaying in this hammock in the grounds of a gorgeous house in Saffron Sweeting, instead of dragging around the Royston shops, like we usually would.

'Right.' I nod and write *How many kids*. Two is best, three would be okay. More, without prior discussion, is scary, and Olivia should know. Her husband, Adrian, works in London and has a tiny studio flat for Sunday to Thursday nights. Then he joins her for the weekend, wherever she's house-sitting. He's not here today, helping a friend buy a car instead. But he's recently told Liv he wants at least four children and she's freaking out, especially given her age.

'What bad dates have you had?' I ask Maddie.

'Oh, I dunno,' she says, in the way people often do, before they start reeling off details. 'A chauvinist, a fascist, a creationist, a zoologist, and two taxi drivers.'

Her logic is inexplicable, but I write the first three down and add *womaniser*.

'Guys who spend more time on their hair than I do.' She leans down from the hammock, plucks a tall piece of grass, and starts to chew on it. 'Oh, and control freaks,' she suggests, when my pencil has caught up.

'Such as?'

'Well, the dude who rearranged the stuff in our dishwasher each time he came over.'

'What, the clean stuff?'

'No, the dirty. He said ours was suboptimal.' She shrugs, clearly still mystified.

But this reminds me. 'Guys like Sebastien, who want a secretary, not a girlfriend.' Six months into our relationship, it was *my* fault he forgot to send his mum a birthday card. 'It was like he transformed from my boyfriend into my boss. When we went to dinner with his best friend and wife, *I* was supposed to buy, write, and send the thank you note.'

'Talking of dinner –' Maddie spits out her grass, '– men who want a cook.'

She can only produce meals involving an electronic gadget, like a bread maker or a slow cooker. Ask her to fry an egg and she's hopeless.

'And if you're eating out,' Olivia adds, 'they should be polite to the waiting staff.'

'Totally,' Maddie confirms. 'It's awful, otherwise.'

'Right.' I add that to my growing list. All three of us have been on the receiving end of cranky customers during waitressing jobs.

I pause, then put *fanatical hobbies* on the next line, doodling swirls on the tail of the 'f'. That one covers a multitude of sins, including the botany student who obsessed over his specimens. 'Do you remember Ken?' I ask my sisters. 'Once autumn came, he dug up all his dahlias and spread the tuber thingies across his bedroom floor. I kept crunching them on my way to the bathroom.'

Olivia shakes her head and laughs, which is refreshing as she usually disapproves of my projects.

'How about you, Liv?' I ask. 'What bad dates have you had?'

She pauses, working her cloth into the awkward corners of a toast rack. For a moment I think she's going to refuse to join in.

But then she grins. 'Well, there was the one I met in a bookshop. I got there early, to browse. He was sitting there trimming his fingernails.'

'What, actually in the store?'

'Yes, in Science Fiction, as I recall.'

Fingernails, I add to my list.

'I could have overlooked that,' she says, with a melancholy sigh. 'It was the rest of it.'

'What did he do?'

'He stared openly at my breasts and asked me, when I last flew out of Stansted, whether the security guy *touched me all over*.'

'Eww.' Maddie and I shrink back in the hammock.

'Oh, and tattoos,' she adds, on a bit of a roll.

I pause. 'What's wrong with tattoos?' I quite like them, in moderation.

'Shows a lack of self-respect. Who would do that to themselves? Oh, and poor ability to plan ahead. Who wants a ninety-year-old husband with tattoos?' This is classic Olivia, always crossing bridges before the river's even flowing.

'Who wants a ninety-year-old husband at all?' Maddie looks repulsed.

'Wait, I've got another,' Olivia says. 'Ask how their last relationship ended. If he says she died, ask how. And if any others have kicked the bucket in mysterious circumstances.'

'Really?' My pencil stops.

'Uh-huh. I once spent thirty minutes in a pub, talking to a guy who claimed two of his previous girlfriends had "simply disappeared".'

'You're kidding. What did you do?'

'I ran out the back and made it three. Jumped on the first bus that was passing and ended up in Hammersmith.'

~ ~ ~

Half an hour later, we're still going.

'Wow,' I say, 'this is really cool.'

'You're never going to date anyone again.' Olivia cranes her neck to peer at my list. 'You're onto two pages.'

'Fine,' I say. 'So be it. Think of all the time I'll save.'

I gaze fondly at the list, starting to embellish it with leaves around the edges.

Maybe, I think, I can take it to a copy shop and get it laminated. Or upload it as a printable to Etsy.

Olivia's phone rings. 'Yep,' she says. 'Hang on a minute.' She hefts up and out of her deckchair. 'Back in a jiff. It's the new gardener, to see about trimming the trees.'

I look up at the branches above us, skittering in the breeze. They seem fine to me. On cue, a wood pigeon lands and begins cooing from its lofty vantage point.

We hear voices in the front garden, then closer, coming through the vegetable patch, or kitchen garden, as Olivia prefers to call it.

'And we thought probably the beech trees, too,' she says, her words carrying as she approaches.

Olivia doesn't walk into a room, she sails in, like a matron in a hospital comedy. No wonder people trust her with their multimillion pound houses.

Behind her strolls a man, silhouetted by the low afternoon sun. I still have one eye on my magnificent list, but I look up as a shadow falls across the hammock.

'Absolutely,' he says, in a rolling accent which sends a zing through me. 'I agree, this is essential.'

He steps closer to examine the trees, and I see he's tall and lithe with tanned olive skin. He's wearing battered jeans, sturdy boots and a worn leather jacket. He's so close I can smell the leather, and aftershave, too.

I look down at my list. Item four: *strong smells*.

'Hello,' says Maddie, from beside me.

I notice she's smiling up at him.

'*Buenas tardes.*' He nods at her and then turns a languid smile on me. 'You ladies are under a very beautiful tree.' He makes those last two words sound as soft as butter.

'This is Javier,' Olivia says, pushing her sunglasses onto her head. 'These are my sisters, Madeline and Alyssa.' To us, she adds, 'He's come to cut the trees,' apparently forgetting she told us that already. Either she's starting to lose her marbles – unlikely – or the gorgeous gardener has rattled her, too.

'But not today,' says Javier. 'Today, I only look.' And look he does, first at Maddie, then me. The light catches the edge of his ears as he shrugs his jacket off and drapes it over the hammock. As he does so, I notice his fingernails are dirty.

Item nine: *weird ears*; item twenty-three: *fingernails*.

Javier takes out his phone and begins snapping photos of the trees.

'Where are you from?' Maddie asks, shooting me a sideways look.

'Sevilla,' he replies. 'That is Seville, to you.' This is barely out of his mouth before I think, eleven: *long distance*.

Then, with a grin, he adds, 'Like Don Juan.'

And possibly item sixteen: *womaniser*.

At this point I notice he has beautiful hair, almost shoulder length, falling back from his face in dark, glossy waves as he assesses the tree. He would indeed make a mesmerising Don Juan on the stage. And the urge to run my hands through item seventeen takes my breath away.

Slowly, I close my sketchbook, tapping my fingers absent-mindedly on the cover.

I could just ask him how many kids he wants, I think, really sink it. Or whether any of his girlfriends have died mysteriously.

'And you specialise in trees?' Maddie speaks up now. 'That's cool.'

'Trees, yes, trees are my first love,' he replies.

Item twenty-two: *fanatical hobbies*.

'But I have to make the ends meet, too. I drive taxi in the evenings, also.'

I catch Maddie roll her eyes and look away.

Taxis, I think. Taxis are fine. Taxis never officially made it onto my list.

'What, *every* evening?' I say. When Javier looks at me, I give him my best smile. 'Surely not?'

'Well, no, Señorita Alyssa,' he admits, with a shrug which shows off strong, working shoulders. 'Not *every* night.'

Surreptitiously, I slide the sketchbook behind my back as I bat my eyelashes a little.

'So... you do have time for... other things?'

Javier leans a hand on the sturdy tree trunk which holds up one end of the hammock. Behind him, Olivia folds her arms and shakes her head.

Fortunately, the gardener from Seville doesn't notice. I think I detect a wink as he looks down at me. '*Sí*, yes, of course I have some time.'

I shift in the hammock and the sketchbook crunches beneath me. 'Well, good.' I ignore it, holding Javier's gaze. 'In fact, I'm delighted to hear it.'

~~~

Author's note: My thanks to reader Connie T. who won my contest to supply words to be woven into a short story. I accepted her challenge of *Madeline Dunbar, Mountain Brook, Alabama, artist,* and *transformed.* This is the result.

Summer Fruits

It was the mountain of plump, shiny gooseberries which first caught Joan's attention. Piled in an old-fashioned wicker basket, each had veins so delicate, they might have been painted on by hand. Then she noticed the man, sitting in the shade, bent over his task. Methodically, he topped and tailed the glossy fruit: *slice, slice,* then dropped them into a huge stainless steel tub at his side – *plink.* He was dressed in chef's whites, but his head was bare, his hair no more than a few wispy strands of grey.

Joan had spent the first part of the morning exploring the walled vegetable garden, where eager beans climbed wigwams to the sky and plump marrows lazed on the soil. The garden was well-tended: patches of damp earth and a faint peaty smell told her the crops had been watered early in the day. The sweet peas had been well-picked, as is necessary, to encourage fresh growth. She wondered who was the lucky recipient of the scented blooms. But as the sun had climbed higher, the imposing orange brick walls had blocked any hint of breeze. Her hip was troubling her; she was in need of a sit-down. Where better than the tea room?

With her handbag slung inelegantly across her body and walking stick hooked awkwardly over one arm, Joan managed to carry her tray outside to the terrace. That's when she saw the fruit, and its handler. From the speed he was working, she hoped the gooseberries weren't intended for today's lunch.

'They're keeping you busy this morning,' Joan said to him as she shuffled by. She never used to start conversations with strangers, but, recently, she'd found entire days could pass in silence.

The chef lifted his head and looked in her general direction. His face was round and weather-beaten. 'It's all I'm good for, these days.'

There was precious little shade on the terrace and Joan didn't fancy the indignity of grappling with one of the furled umbrellas. A small round table next to him was vacant.

'I'm going to sit here in the cool, if you don't mind.' She leaned her stick against the stone building before lowering herself carefully towards a narrow wooden chair. Her joints shrieked and she had to allow gravity to handle the last couple of inches. Fortunately, the chair held. One of these days, it wouldn't.

'You help yourself, my dear.' He reached for a cloth to wipe his fingers. It was lying on the table next to his hand, but it took him a couple of pats to find it.

Joan looked more closely, nodding as she understood. He was almost blind.

She poured a careful splash of milk into her cup, then added the tea, served, as it should be, in a proper china pot. 'It's going to be another scorcher.'

'It is,' he agreed. 'I don't know who's going to want a hot pudding on a day like this, but there you have it.'

'Are they going in a pie, then?' She sipped her tea gratefully.

'Crumble. So I'm told.' *Slice, slice, plink.* 'I don't decide the menu, not any more.'

Again, he looked in her direction and she saw his cloudy eyes. Cataracts, almost certainly.

'But you used to plan what to cook?'

'I've worked here since before the house was given over to the National Trust,' he said. 'Before the family ran into problems, couldn't pay the inheritance tax. It was a different place, back then.'

Joan had the luxury of being able to observe, without him knowing she was staring. She guessed he was in his seventies too. Apart from his eyes, he seemed to be in good health.

'Oh yes, I've cooked for the rich and famous,' he continued. 'Made lunch for Elizabeth Taylor, once. Trout, it was. Trout with almonds.' He stared off into the distance for a few moments before resuming his work. His fingers were still nimble, just slow.

'But now you can't cook, because of your eyes?'

'That's right, lass. A blind chef isn't much use to anyone.'

She liked being called *lass*. That hadn't happened in a long time. 'Have you had your cataracts looked at?'

'Oh, no. Nobody's taking a paring knife to my eyeballs.' He sniffed. 'I don't trust hospitals. Too many folk die in those places.'

Joan laughed. 'I don't think they do.'

'My mother died, for starters. Having me.'

'I'm sorry.' She coughed awkwardly.

He shrugged. 'My father never forgave me.'

'It was hardly your fault.'

'No. But he never came to terms with it. He couldn't talk about her, drunk or sober. I spent the next forty years trying to apologise for being born.'

'Then what happened?'

'He died.'

Joan said nothing, but drank her tea and listened to the steady rhythm of his work. The *plink* of falling gooseberries had changed to a *plunk*: he had filled the bottom layer of the tub.

'Then, there was Billy Morse,' he continued. 'The boys at school, they either ignored me, or poked fun. Being ignored was better, obviously. I got by just fine with no friends: found a corner of the playground and kept my head down. But one day, out of the blue, Billy Morse shared his lunch. There was never much food around at my house, you see. I had to find it myself, or go hungry.'

That made sense, with no mother and a father gone to pieces.

'Yes, Billy scuffed up to me in his short trousers, sat down and offered me half his ham sandwich.' *Slice, slice, plunk.* 'We were friends for life.'

Joan poured extra hot water into the pot and hassled the bag with her teaspoon. Loose leaves would have been preferable, but one couldn't have everything.

'Last winter, they took Billy into hospital for his prostate. Routine, they said. A couple of days, they said.'

She murmured, so he would know she was listening.

'You won't get me near those places now.' He stopped slicing for several seconds.

'I'm sorry about your mother and your friend,' Joan said. 'But I can tell you, hospitals aren't as dangerous as all that.'

'Hmmph. What are you then, a doctor?'

'No, a nurse,' she said crisply. 'Retired, I mean.'

'And I suppose you worked with eyes.'

'No, paediatrics.'

She hadn't started off in paediatrics. That was the most popular ward, and Joan wasn't pretty or funny or persuasive, like the other new nurses. So they sent her to oncology. There, she witnessed white pain and dark suffering that twisted her stomach and sent her running to the toilet to retch. After the first year, she learned to see without remembering, to touch without feeling, her emotions for her patients as starched as her uniform.

Joan's thirty-seventh birthday turned into thirty-eight and then thirty-nine, and she still hadn't had a child. Fred stammered words of comfort, but the gap in their family threatened to swallow her. She went to the hospital administrators and told them that unless they transferred her to paediatrics, she would leave and train as a teacher. Within three months, they moved her to a children's ward and that's where she stayed for the next two decades.

'I saw hundreds of operations,' Joan told her gooseberry friend. 'I know what I'm talking about.'

'And how many of them died?'

'Not many.' She paused. 'Well, not many who weren't going to die in any case.'

He chuckled. 'Thanks, but no thanks.'

Joan pursed her lips but changed the topic. 'I just came from the walled garden. Beautiful-looking vegetables.'

He nodded. 'Yes, it's a fine plot. A grand kitchen garden. I used to stroll down there in the early evening and eye up what might be ready the following day. In summer, this estate was darn near self-sufficient.'

Joan thought of the pitiful tomato plants in the back garden of her house, the home Fred and she had bought when they were first married. Her vegetable bed was growing more weeds than food this year. Darned hip. She'd waited stubbornly until it was unbearable, before seeking help. Foolish mistake.

'What's your favourite dish to cook?' she asked him. 'If you could, I mean.'

'Ah, that's easy.' He smiled. 'Game pie.'

'Game pie?'

'From scratch. Rabbit, venison, pheasant. Carrots, potatoes, pastry, everything from scratch. I'd prepare the game myself. No shortcuts.'

'I don't often see that on menus, these days.'

'No, folks are too squeamish to make it – or too lazy, I don't know which. But I bake a wonderful game pie. Of course, you have to plan ahead.'

'And it's not really a dish for a day like today.' Joan's patch of shade was shrinking and she scraped her chair back a fraction.

'No, no, it's an autumn dish, winter, even. October, November, when the nights are getting chilly and there's mist in the air. November's best.'

He paused in his work, his head lifted, as if he were looking out across the estate, to where the deer were grazing peacefully.

'You know,' Joan waited a few moments and then said carefully, 'I need a hip replacement and there's a six-month waiting list. My vegetable plot will be a jungle when I eventually get back to it.'

'I'm sorry to hear it,' he said.

'The wait's much shorter, for cataracts.' She hoped she was right. 'You'd see your GP, who'd send you to a specialist, and then they'd probably do it in day surgery. You'd be in and out in less time than it's taking you to humiliate those gooseberries.'

'You're a cheeky lass.' He gave a chuckle.

Joan finished her tea and gathered her things together. She found her stick, then hoisted herself up, using the edge of the wobbly table for support.

'Who knows, you might be making game pie this autumn,' she said.

'I might,' he said slowly. 'I might.'

'Well, I'll look for it on the menu, then. In November.'

As she hobbled away, she tried to read his expression. But with his eyes so foggy, there were no clues, just the gentle nodding of his head in time with his work.

Slice, slice, plunk.

~~~

Author's note: *Summer Fruits* was originally published in *Toasted Cheese Literary Journal.*

Teapot

This party was a huge mistake. The guy in the hat is clearly deranged. And the girl in blue looked friendly, but hasn't stopped arguing. I'm yawning profusely and if it wasn't for that heavenly aroma of cake, I'd have scampered ages ago.

'You're leaving, Alice?' The hatted eccentric is momentarily distracted by the grumpy girl's departure.

I seize my chance, pouncing for the teapot lid. Then I prise it up and wriggle. As I drop down into the dark sanctuary, the comforting clink of china sounds above my head.

The hatted voice is reduced to a distant rumble. 'Where did the dormouse go?'

Alone at last.

~~~

Author's note: This is both flash fiction, aiming to tell a complete story in around a hundred words, and fan fiction, best enjoyed by those who have read *Alice's Adventures in Wonderland*. This piece was originally published at julievalerie.com.

Checking In

From behind the reception desk, Pete hands me a shiny key and gestures to a man waiting quietly nearby. 'This is Gabe,' he says. 'He'll show you to your room.'

Gabe steps forward. His skin is dark mahogany, the whites of his eyes two bright spots in his face. Then he smiles, and his beautiful teeth steal the show.

'You've had a long journey, Miss Hamilton,' he says. 'You must be tired.'

That's an understatement: I'm wrecked. Every limb aches and my head throbs. When I nod in response, my neck feels like it's been twisted all the way around, like an owl's.

'Would you like me to call for a golf buggy?' Gabe reads my body language.

'That's okay.' I don't know why I refuse. 'I can walk.'

They sent my bag to the room while I was checking in. From that process, I can tell the resort is laid-back, casual, but crisply efficient. They knew who I was, almost before I walked through the ornate gates, past the bougainvillea, and into the lobby cooled by ceiling fans. Perhaps I'm the only single female arriving today. Or they know the flight times and guessed when I would reach the hotel. I don't know. But Pete barely glanced at my passport. I'm not even sure he bothered to run my credit card.

'It gets dark in about an hour,' Gabe says, leading the way across the lobby, which is open on one side to offer a glimpse of the pool and palm trees beyond. 'Good that you arrived in daylight.'

We step outside, onto a path that winds among lush foliage. Beyond the pool, where a few guests bask in the slowly lowering sun, I can see the beach and hear the waves breaking gently on the shore. There's a breeze from that direction, and a chirping from some small birds with bright tufts on their heads.

'These are our standard rooms.' Gabe gestures to a whitewashed block, facing the pool, three storeys high.

'Very nice.' I assume that's the category of accommodation I booked. How can I not know that? It must be my headache, messing with my cognitive processes.

'Whereas, we've allocated you a superior suite.' Once again, Gabe guesses my thoughts.

'Oh.' I'm pretty sure I didn't reserve that. I can already tell this place is more luxurious than anywhere I usually stay, so there's no way I would have splurged on a posh room. Why can't I remember? What's wrong with me today? Should I say something, or keep quiet? Perhaps they're full and have upgraded me.

We turn a corner and pass behind a low restaurant building. Twenty or so tables are arranged on its verandah, facing the ocean. They're set for dinner, with wine glasses and pale blue napkins. I sniff the air, wondering what's cooking, but all I get is a fruity scent which could be either from the gardens, or the guests' sunscreen.

Gabe sees where I'm looking. 'Dinner starts at six,' he says. 'Not long to wait. You have a choice of two restaurants tonight. Soft drinks and house wine are included.'

I don't remember any of these details from choosing this place. This must be costing an arm and a leg. I'm sure I can't afford it, not with last month's rent increase, and the tighter commissions at work.

'Uhh...' I want to ask him about my reservation, but feel foolish. Surely I should have clarified that with Pete, at the front desk? Shouldn't he have given me something to sign, with the room rate on it? Did I complete any paperwork? Think, Rachel, *think*.

'Most people, of course, get the standard room.' Gabe strolls easily beside me. His uniform is a white linen shirt and khaki trousers, elegant but practical. 'A few, I'm sorry to say, end up over there.'

I look where he's pointing, but all I see are tennis courts, flanked by dense bushes. Some low roofs, however, are visible beyond.

'Over there?'

He nods. 'Or at a different... resort... entirely.'

I have no clue what he means. 'Surely people just get what they booked?' I ask.

He laughs. 'That's an excellent way of putting it. Yes, I suppose they do.'

Why did he find that funny? I open my mouth to say something else, but he's pointing again.

'Now, here's our spa. We call it Cloud – we'll get you in there tomorrow. You look like death warmed up, if you don't mind me saying.'

Normally, I would mind. I would mind enormously. As a single woman in my late twenties, who sells dental products for a living, I take my appearance seriously. But he's right.

Gabe pauses on a little bridge which connects a lazy river with another swimming pool. 'This is our adults-only pool.'

The pool is deserted, the water barely lapping at the edges. It looks heavenly. 'I haven't actually seen many kids.' I frown, working hard to recall the other guests we passed only minutes ago.

Gabe sucks in his breath. 'Just the way we like it. It's terrible, really, when the wee ones come.' He shakes his head. 'Upsets all of us, even the old-timers.'

I raise my eyebrows. I'm not much of a kid person myself – plenty of time for that, I reckon, once I turn thirty and meet the right man – but his attitude seems a bit extreme for someone who works in tourism.

'But happily,' Gabe says, showing me his perfect molars, 'we've not had any recently.'

Okay, that really is weird. He's more eccentric than he looks.

'This is our cocktail bar: Gates. And on the upper deck, our seafood restaurant.' Gabe's gesturing again. He's clearly proud of this place. 'Reservations are essential – call the front desk and say you want to dine at Pearl.'

Hmm, they like to give things one-word names here. Well, I suppose it makes life easy.

'And there, on the beach, are our luxury suites.' He places both hands on his hips and raises his chin as he looks proudly towards the sand.

I see a series of individual thatched huts, facing the sea. Even from here, they look amazing.

'Wow,' I say, 'those are on my bucket list, for sure.'

Gabe throws his head back and laughs again. 'I love your sense of humour!' he says, before clapping me on the back. I wince but he doesn't notice. 'Bucket list! Hah!' He puts his head on one side, considering me. 'You're going to do fine,' he says. 'I can tell.'

What the heck does that mean?

'So, I bet you've got rich and famous folk staying in those, right?' I ask, as we begin walking again, now on a path which runs parallel to the ocean, along the back of the luxury huts.

'Hmmph,' is the unexpected reply. 'Famous, yes. Rich... not so much.'

I look at him questioningly.

'We've had Nelson Mandela, yes. And Mother Teresa. She had that last cottage, there.'

'Wow.'

Gabe must be older than he looks, if he's worked here that long. Mother Teresa's been dead for years.

'Mmm, yes, and that nurse – what was her name? Flo... Florence someone.'

'Nightingale,' I say, reflexively, then wait for him to praise my humour again.

'Nightingale! That's the one. Nice lady.'

I look at him. He's totally pulling my leg. What an oddball.

But he's still straight-faced. 'Not far now.'

The path turns away from the beach, through another lush garden, and emerges in a pretty courtyard. Five tiny cottages are arranged around it, each with their own front porch and hammock.

'Oh!' I stop, charmed. 'How lovely.'

Gabe strides towards the cottage in the far corner, more set back than the others. In addition to the hammock, a cobalt-painted rocking chair sits on the porch. The front door is also blue. Like the beach cottages, the roof is thatched.

Gabe gestures to the key I'm carrying. 'Miss Hamilton, may I have the honour?'

'Please do.' I drop it into his hand.

Inside, the cottage is cool. The shutters are closed, the ceiling fan is on, and I sense air conditioning too. We step into one large room, with a huge bed near the door and a pair of chic sofas at the other end. The walls are soft white, the bedding is white, the furniture is white. The orchid on the console table is white. A pale blue quilt, and an abstract cerulean painting which could be sea, or sky, or both, offer the only colour in the space.

'How... serene.' I look around, then perch on the bed as the calm reaches out and swaddles me. 'It's lovely.'

'I'm glad you like it.' Gabe starts to say something else, but my attention is captured by the television. It's on, not surprising in an upmarket hotel like this, and I assume it's the welcome channel, promoting the resort's facilities.

But within moments, I see this video loop is altogether more personal.

'That's me!' My mouth drops open at a wobbly shot of me, around age ten, on a pony. My mother walks alongside, one hand steadying me in the saddle.

'Is that –? That's my graduation,' I say, recognising my friends from university giggling alongside me, all of us twirling the tassels on our ludicrous mortarboard hats. I clamber off the bed to put my nose closer to the screen. I must have misplaced my contact lenses, somewhere on the trip.

'Why is the TV showing – oh God, that dress was awful.' It's switched now to the wedding of a childhood friend. I was chief bridesmaid and wore lilac flounces. 'This is... bizarre.'

Gabe stands, head on one side, watching the screen. 'Don't you like it? It's quite popular. We call it Eulogy Tube.'

'You... Did you say Eulogy?'

Gabe doesn't answer. Nor does he look away from the television. 'Ah,' he says finally, 'here it is.'

'That's not me,' I say, as a more professional clip comes on. It looks like the local news programme. 'Definitely not me.' The woman on camera is glamorous, polished, blonde.

'The funeral of Rachel Hamilton was held today in her home town of St Albans. Miss Hamilton, who was killed last week on a pedestrian crossing in the town centre, has been hailed a heroine for saving eighteen-month-old twins from a speeding bus. Police confirmed today that the bus driver suffered a heart attack and they are waiting to interview him in hospital. The family of Mabel and Mimi Braithwaite praised Miss Hamilton for pushing their pram clear of the bus, leaving herself in its path.'

'What is this?' I sit back heavily on the squishy bed. 'What's... going on?'

My jet lag must be catching up with me, big time. My whole head is foggy. This doesn't make sense. Why is a montage of clips from my life on the resort television? What the hell was that last one?

'Gabe?' I look up at him as he clicks the television off, then crosses to the windows to tilt the shutters. Slanted light dances into the room.

'Gabe!' I say again, panic rising through my voice. 'Where am I?'

'Miss Hamilton... Rachel...' he says. 'I thought... that you were doing so well.'

'Well? What do you mean, well?'

'I thought... you understood. I'm so sorry, I thought you knew. I should have explained.'

'What do you mean?' My tongue repeats, as my stumbling brain thinks, no, actually, don't explain. I don't want to hear this.

I flop back on the bed, my aching limbs begging for sleep. Above me, against the white ceiling, the fan spins slowly enough for me to follow an individual blade, if I try. I let my eyes circle for a few moments, already wrapped in the blissful calm of this place. Pearl... Gates... Peter.

The fog dissolves.

Slowly, I puff the air out through my stinging lungs, then drag my torso up, propping on my elbows to consider Gabe. He's still by the window.

'The rooms people get,' I say, speaking now with effort. 'Standard or... superior. You... allocate them, don't you?'

Gabe nods.

'But not based on what they pay,' I continue.

'Oh, it's a form of payment, Miss Hamilton. Just... a different currency.'

'And I'm in here because...' I can barely say it. 'Because of... those twins.'

He nods again.

'And your name isn't really Gabe, is it?'

He raises his eyebrows. 'It is, miss, yes. Absolutely.'

I shake my head, which thumps obligingly. 'But you've shortened it, haven't you?' No wonder my entire body screams each time I move. *I was hit by a bus.* 'What does... what does your mother call you?'

The last sunlight of the day nudges its way in, creating a halo effect behind him.

'Ah, yes, Miss Hamilton, well... my friends all call me Gabe. Have done for years.' He grins now, a wonderful, angelic smile. 'But my mother, she likes to call me Gabriel.'

On the Shelf

I can't believe it. Just days after Thanksgiving, mere weeks before Christmas, and I'm technically homeless. Sean wouldn't look me in the eye as he told me I had to go. Although I knew we had ended up together more by default than because he loved me, I didn't expect it to come to this.

So here I am, back on the shelf, and a dark, dusty one at that, with the other losers and society's cast-offs. We're all looking sorrowful, although some are more stoic than others. The fact is, each of us has been passed over, in favour of younger versions.

I should be able to hold my head high. I have good bones, great breeding. My face is attractive, classic, my full mouth curving just the right amount. And I've always loved the elegant slenderness of my waist. Below that, it's true, things aren't so sexy – I flare out from the hips down – but that's a simple necessity, for balance.

I've been stuck in this stale, hushed place for two days now and haven't said more than a quick *hello* to my neighbours. The guy on my right is gloomy, taciturn. He welcomed me with little more than a grunt. On my left, well, she might be pretty, if she'd only stop sobbing. I admit, I got a bit tearful myself in the chill of the first night, but that's no way to carry on. Reality has to be faced.

'I'm Gus. Sorry, didn't catch your name.' The right-hand guy speaks suddenly.

'Rose.' I glance at him. He's much older than me, heavily built, with strong features. Chiselled, you could say.

'Welcome to Dumpsville, Rose. Rejects and broken hearts unite.'

'I'm only here temporarily,' I tell him.

'Sure you are.'

I mean it: of course I'll escape this cheap, musty thrift store. I started off so well in life, this must be a blip.

I was purchased as an expensive wedding gift from a high-end retail shop, in the days before it turned all industrial and started selling coffee tables made out of factory junk. True, I was probably made in China or Korea, but I was too young to remember that.

My first real home was with Diana and Ricky, a charming couple, buoyantly in love. But the marriage ended after just three years, when Ricky had a non-virtual affair with his virtual assistant. Diana gave me, along with her prettiest wedding china, to her sister, Corrine.

I was concerned, I won't pretend otherwise. Corrine was young, barely out of her teens, and my graceful looks border on traditional. But it turned out okay. She brought me out regularly to display sweetly scented flowers from her boyfriend, the good-looking but irresponsible Sean. I watched with interest from my sunny windowsill as their relationship matured: Sean settled down and got a steady job in a bookstore.

'I heard you crying last night,' Gus says.

Nosy devil. It's bad enough we're all squashed up here on the top shelf together, no privacy, without him getting impertinent. 'Just a bit homesick,' I tell him.

'Look, it's not so bad here. Keep your nose clean and stay out of trouble.'

'What kind of trouble?'

'Well, there's her, for a start. Marsha. Runs the place.' He indicates an overweight woman, spilling uncomfortably off a stool behind the cash register. She's flicking through a gossip magazine, but I've spotted her stealing outside for a cigarette, whenever the store is empty. Then she sprays a lily of the valley perfume on her cleavage to mask the smell.

'She's nasty,' Gus continues. 'She'll drop you deliberately, just to get rid of you.'

'She would do that?' I look in horror at Gus. A square, chunky whisky decanter, he isn't my type, but I can see some women would find him attractive. He needs a good wash, though.

'Yes. Once you're damaged, she gives you two weeks on the bargain shelf, then, out you go.' He nods his glass stopper meaningfully.

'That's horrible.' I start to feel worried. 'How long have you been here?'

Gus shrugs. 'I dunno. Not that long. A few months, maybe?'

A few months? Surely it won't take more than a week or two for someone to purchase me?

'Then, of course, there's the danger of being bought,' Gus says.

'What do you mean? That's wonderful! Isn't that what we all want, a home?' I look around the shop at the straggling inmates, picturing how much happier we'd all be with a real family to love us.

'Not as simple as that, these days. See him?' Gus points to a large, framed canvas, being carried to the front of the shop by a wiry, intense woman in white jeans. As they pass, I see a brown, heavy scene of dogs in a library.

'The painting?' I ask.

'Yes, him, the one showing off because he thinks he's got a first class ticket out of here. Poor sucker. He'll be painted over before Monday.'

'Painted over?'

'For sure. She doesn't want the picture, just the canvas. She might keep the frame, if he's lucky, but I doubt it.'

'Oh, my gosh. I had no idea.'

'You don't need to worry too much.' Gus looks me up and down. 'There's not much they can do to you. Spray paint, maybe. The mercury glass look is in, especially for the holidays.'

Spray me? Good Lord above. I don't know what to say and go pale. Did Sean suspect my fate when he dropped me off last weekend, squashed into a bag with a bunch of VHS tapes and a few old sweaters?

It hadn't lasted, him and Corinne. The more he grew up, the more she seemed to miss her wild, unreliable boyfriend. I was needed less and less for displaying flowers. Eventually, Corrine announced she was going to Australia and, with just two suitcases, took a taxi to the airport. Sean, tight-lipped and angry, existed on beers and microwave meals for a couple of months. Then he started clearing out her stuff, making more space for his books.

Gus rambles on tactlessly. 'You'll probably be okay. It's the wooden furniture you have to feel sorry for.'

'Why?' I follow his gaze to the assortment of tables and nightstands in the corner. They're gathered respectfully around a glass-doored china cabinet. Solidly constructed of teak and oak, they seem like a noble bunch.

'They're gonna get painted. Dead certainty. Take Nigel, last week. I didn't have the heart to tell him, he was so thrilled when he was picked.'

'What do you mean, *painted?*'

'You know, duck-egg blue, pale grey. Bright orange, in some cases. Nobody wants wood any more.'

'Really?' I'm shocked. 'How ugly.'

'But it's not just the painting.' Gus grimaces. 'They'll get sanded, too. At least once, maybe twice.' He lowers his voice. 'I saw it once. There was a special machine, whirring so loud it drowned out the screams. Poor chair was in agony.'

I feel sick. Sanding? With a machine? How can that be legal?

I open my mouth to say more, but Gus shushes me. I hadn't noticed the little boy and his father approaching our row.

The boy points to an ornate china urn. 'This is pretty.' He's wearing a red coat, mittens dangling from the sleeves by elastic. He can't be more than eight years old.

Gus sniggers.

'What?' I whisper.

'That's Fernando.' Gus talks in an undertone. 'He got donated by mistake. We're all taking bets on how long until they come back for him.'

The father lifts Fernando's lid, then sucks in a breath before dropping it with a clunk. 'No way, Charlie,' he says.

'I don't understand,' I hiss.

'Ashes, dummy,' Gus whispers back. 'The family moved and someone donated Grandpa.'

I fight an inappropriate urge to giggle. They're coming nearer.

'But you said I could buy something for Mommy. For under the tree,' Charlie protests. 'With my own money.' He's clutching a handful of crumpled dollar bills.

'Pick something else, buddy.' His father yawns.

Charlie stops dead in front of Gus and me, his brow furrowed. I freeze.

'I want this vase,' the boy announces, looking up at our high shelf. 'She's shiny.'

The father appraises me doubtfully. 'Are you sure?'

Charlie nods. 'Mommy will like her.'

'It, not her.' His dad corrects him. 'It's a vase.'

At that moment, the father's cell phone rings, slicing the stale silence in the shop.

'Help me!' I cry to Gus, during the brief diversion. 'I'm scared.'

'I can't, Rose.' He shakes his stopper head. 'Anyway, this is good.'

'Is it?' I can't breathe, looking in terror at the man's broad back.

'Yes,' Gus says. 'It's great. A Christmas gift for Mom from her little boy, that's as good as it gets.'

The phone call is over. Large hands grip me by the waist and pull me down. For a moment, I am giddy, airborne, then I'm tucked under the father's arm.

'Good luck,' Gus calls from on high.

'Thanks. You too,' I shoot back, as I'm marched towards Marsha and her cash till. Charlie trots alongside, beaming.

I cast a fearful look back at Gus. He tilts his head to me in farewell and then I fix my eyes resolutely ahead.

For better or worse, to be painted or not, I'm going home for the holidays.

~~~

Author's note: Originally published under the title *Thrift Store* in *House of Fifty* magazine.

Attention Span

Becky slogged up the last few stairs to her flat, balanced by a sagging bag of groceries in each hand. The thin plastic handles cut into her fingers, matching the pinching of the ankle strap on her right shoe. The narrow red brick building, slotted in neatly between a launderette and a fish and chip shop, was far too old to have a lift. But the daily stair climbing kept her calves in shape and Becky knew she paid a hundred pounds less in rent each month than the three Lebanese waiters who shared the space below.

Her landlady, Mrs Cargyle, wasn't mean, just old. She lived two streets away with three near-identical terriers and a Great Dane, but didn't get out much. She tended to be absent-minded about scheduling maintenance, including window cleaning. As a result, Becky's flat was darker than it should have been, but at least the top floor did catch the breeze during the muggy August nights which passed for summer in Bethnal Green. Now, though, in October, the draughts were more of a problem.

It might be time to look seriously for a new job, Becky thought, as she nudged her key into the wobbly Yale lock of flat four. She'd hoped to become an architect, not waste her days taking messages, arranging long tubes of site plans, and ordering stationery supplies. Martin could be such a drama queen when someone nicked his beloved brand of pencil. You'd think he was about to paint the Sistine Chapel, she thought, using her backside to nudge the door shut behind her, not sketch a conservatory in Barking.

With a grateful exhale, she lowered the shopping bags to the floor, wriggling her foot from the pesky shoe at the same time. The flat was decidedly chilly: maybe she should bleed the radiators again. Becky flicked on the light. Nothing happened.

She sighed and hobbled, still wearing one shoe, towards the kitchen. The hall lights had been okay, so if the kitchen light wasn't working either, probably a fuse had blown. This was not unusual, as the electrics were roughly the same age as Mrs Cargyle. But Becky's dad had – cautiously – presented her with a toolbox for her twenty-fifth birthday in April, and she'd been tackling more and more of these irritations herself.

'Didn't want you to get your hopes up that it was full of make-up,' he'd said, after she'd removed the red bow from the shiny silver case with reinforced corners.

'No, no, it's great.' Becky had kept her face bent over the box, buying time by examining the different layers of screwdrivers, spanners, pliers, picture hooks, and fuse wire. It was quite a contrast to the silk dress and matching cashmere shawl of four years ago, chosen by her mum. Still, who needed silk dresses to crawl around under the big desks of the architect's office? What good was a cashmere shawl when the internet router had to be reset? 'Maybe you can teach me what to do with it all?' she'd suggested to her father, whose relief was visible. It was important they spend time together, find something in common, now they were a family of two.

Halfway to the kitchen, Becky tripped over something. Already unbalanced by her single shoe, she found herself nose down on Mrs Cargyle's grey, fusty carpet. At least, it was grey now. Becky had never liked to ponder what colour it had started out.

'Oof,' came a female grumble. 'You gone and woke me.'

'What was that?' said another girlish voice.

'Oh, she's home!' This, Becky was sure, was a third person, also female, and young.

Becky sat up as, behind her, someone switched one of the living room lamps on. Not a fuse, then, was her first thought, her brain choosing to process the mundane detail first. Several microseconds later, the bizarre scene registered.

Peering down at her from their perches on every piece of furniture, were girls. Pale-skinned girls, some short, some tall, but all skinny, with huge white eyes. They wore the same clothing: bottle-green pleated skirts, white shirts, and white knee-high socks.

'Who the hell are you?' Becky scrambled up, shock grappling with indignation. 'Why are you in my house?'

They weren't Carmela's friends, surely? Becky's flatmate, a quiet young woman from Madrid, worked part-time as a nanny in Stoke Newington. Most evenings, the curvy Spaniard played poker, consistently fooling the other players with her innocent appearance. The result, Becky knew, was a five-figure investment tucked away in a FTSE tracker fund.

'She won't hurt us, will she, Maria?' One of the smaller girls nudged closer to her larger neighbour, a teenager whose shirt strained across her chest. The rest of the group, making a total of five draped over seats plus three on the floor, watched in silent wariness. The one whose feet, or legs, had tripped Becky up, drew her limbs back into the smallest possible space.

Something about their guarded faces and piercing gazes made Becky pause.

'No,' she said, removing her hands from her hips. 'I just want to know who you are. Are you with Carmela?' Silence. 'Are you from Spain?'

The teenager – Maria – put her arm around the smaller girl. 'We're from Romania,' she said.

Bloody hell, thought Becky. Refugees? Brought here in the secret compartment of a container lorry and tipped out on Hackney Road to fend for themselves? That Yale lock was more useless than she thought.

'You said you'd help us,' said the tripper, from the floor.

'I what?' Becky gaped at her.

'You did,' confirmed Maria, who was clearly the group leader.

'Er, no.' Becky folded her arms now. 'And I'm, umm, sorry, but you have to go. All of you.' For some reason, her eyes went to the bags of groceries. She wasn't about to try to feed nine people with a loaf of bread, three apples, two tins of baked beans, a pint of milk, and six loo rolls. 'Now,' she added. Then, because she was British, after all, 'Sorry.'

'You absolutely promised to help us. I read it.' Maria's hair was cropped unusually close to her head, in a style, Becky saw now, they all shared.

'Where?' Becky, outnumbered, was on the defensive. 'When?'

'On Facebook.' Maria raised her chin infinitesimally.

'You said it was an outrage and that the world should be ashamed,' said a girl on the floor.

'And that you'd help us get home.' This came from an intruder perched on the arm of the sofa.

'Hang on. I don't understand.' Becky looked from one to another. 'You want to go home?' This wasn't normal, surely, for refugees, to want to go back so soon?

'Of course we do. We were kidnapped.' Maria's voice betrayed exasperation that Becky was being so dim. 'We miss our families.'

'Jesus Christ. You're the Romanian schoolgirls!'

Half the uninvited guests made 'duh, obvious' gestures, while the others drew back a little.

'There's no need to use the Lord's name like that,' Maria said. 'But yes, we are. Some of them.'

'I don't understand. How are you –?' Becky's hand was over her mouth. 'When did you –?' She stopped. These girls had been the talk of social media for, what, ten days? Two weeks? Becky's entire social network had been appalled at their kidnapping, had shared and tweeted and pinned and commented with gusto. Becky remembered now, she'd been so caught up in it, she'd completely forgotten to buy biscuits for the Tuesday staff meeting.

'And you said you'd do everything in your power to get us home again.'

'It's there, on your Facebook profile.' The small timid one was gaining confidence.

'I don't believe it.' Becky shook herself. 'How can this...?' She took a faltering step back, trying to put distance between herself and her eight uninvited guests. But in the cramped flat, it was futile. 'All right,' she said instead. 'I'll make a cup of tea.'

If not an answer, that was at least a reasonable gesture. It would help with the shock, for starters, and as far as Becky knew, offering tea was a sign of hospitality in most cultures. But did she have eight spare mugs?

She stepped into the kitchen, which was little more than an alcove off the living room. The light switch, thankfully, cooperated, but Becky took one look at the scene it revealed, and smacked it off again. She half turned back to the assembled schoolgirls, then took a deep breath before trying the kitchen light again.

'Mother of –' Just in time, she stopped herself from blaspheming again.

A seven-foot model of the Eiffel Tower took up the entire floor space, its legs splaying to the fridge, the window, the oven, and the recycling bin. Becky had only visited Paris once but as far as she could tell, it was an accurate miniature, with three levels, intricate crisscross ironwork, and little staircases at the corners. Bizarrely, perched on the horizontal parts, were vegetables: carrots, broccoli, cauliflower. Courgettes were stuffed in some of the smaller gaps, while a marrow teetered above Becky's head. Tomatoes decorated the highest parts, and she spotted a glossy purple aubergine.

'Who put that there? And what the hell's with the veggies?'

If she'd expected an answer from the schoolgirls, none was forthcoming.

'This is ridiculous.' Becky tried to squeeze past the Eiffel Tower to reach the kettle, and found it was impossible, at least not without dislodging several cucumbers.

Aware her heart rate was rising, she decided to seek refuge in the bathroom. Surely that wasn't full of girls or gourds?

It wasn't. It was worse. In the bathtub was a lion, his impressive mane a little bedraggled, standing patiently while a woman in a grey pinstripe skirt suit and patent court shoes hosed him down with the handheld shower attachment.

Becky gave an audible yelp, followed by an 'oh' as she realised the lion was bleeding from a wound on his back.

'Don't worry,' said the woman, reaching for Becky's chamomile shampoo. 'He's harmless.'

'He doesn't look harmless.' Becky should have asked who she was, where the lion had come from, and why he was being hosed down in her bath. But her stare was glued on the beast as he gave a small yawn, exposing two neat rows of deadly weapons.

'Cedric knows you're a friend.' The woman gave the feline a pat, before aiming the shower head to rinse around the edges of the bath. Becky could see diluted blood running to the drain.

'He's hurt,' she blurted. Surely animals attack more readily when they feel vulnerable?

'Just a scratch. Lucky for Cedric, the wally had terrible aim.'

Becky sagged against the doorway now, not even murmuring a protest as Cedric's bath attendant grabbed Becky's favourite fluffy towel – the cream one, of course – and began rubbing his mane gently. Then she looked up.

'Oh, you're a wee bit nonplussed, are you?'

'I... I really don't understand.' Becky would have liked to flee back to the relative safety of the Eiffel Tower, but her legs wouldn't comply. 'Who on earth are you all? And why are you in my flat. Did... Carmela send you?' Could this be a poker bet gone wrong?

The woman threw the now sodden towel on the floor, stood upright, and stretched.

'Carmela? No. We're your feed, of course.'

'My... my what?'

'Your Facebook feed. Your social media.' She stuck out a hand. 'I'm Fey, nice to meet you.'

'There must be a mistake,' Becky said, even as she shook Fey's hand out of reflexive politeness. Why did everyone keep talking about Facebook today? 'I don't know any of you.'

'But you do, silly!' Fey gave Cedric one more pat. The lion shook himself, and to Becky's horror, looked like he was considering a leap from the bath. Instead, he sat down where he was, and raised a front paw to lick it. Becky breathed again.

'Look, come and sit down,' said Fey, then, as Becky didn't argue, led the way back to the living room.

Obligingly, two of the Romanian schoolgirls shifted from the sofa, one of them sliding to the floor and the other leaning against the small dining table Carmela had squeezed in next to the wall.

'We're your feed,' Fey said again. 'All the things you said you're passionate about.'

'I'm not passionate about you,' Becky said, her eyes darting around the room. If anything, she felt more trapped than she had in the bathroom, with a four hundred pound lion close enough to touch.

Maria tutted. 'We've been through this,' she said. 'Everything in your power to get us home. You promised.'

Becky looked at Fey, not so much for support as to avoid Maria's intense scrutiny.

'She's right.' Fey nodded and sat back.

'And – the – the lion?' Becky's voice rose.

'Cedric? Oh, he's Cecil's brother. You remember Cecil, don't you? You were so indignant when he was shot.'

Cecil the lion. Becky closed her eyes briefly. Yes, that had been awful. Some American tourist paid a few thousand dollars for an excursion to exterminate one of earth's most majestic creatures. She had been up in arms, so to speak, over that. They all had been.

'You tweeted that you wouldn't rest until animals like Cecil were protected,' said Fey.

'That wasn't just me,' Becky protested. 'Everyone was outraged.' Even Martin had spent that morning reading out bits from the newspaper. Nor had he complained when Becky spent the afternoon clicking online petitions and sending links to her friends.

'It's good you were outraged,' Fey smiled. 'But then what did you *do* about it?'

'What do you mean, do about it?'

Becky remembered her two bags of shopping were still sitting by the front door, but this didn't seem a good moment to retrieve them. Anyway, she couldn't get to the fridge.

'You didn't do anything to follow through, did you?' Fey said. 'You forgot about it.'

'I didn't,' lied Becky.

'Yes, you did. Your attention span doesn't last more than two minutes.'

'Which is bad,' said one of the Romanian girls.

'So, you're – what? Here to remind me?' This wasn't the evening Becky had envisaged at all. She'd far rather be lying under a radiator with a spanner right now. And she still hadn't had that cup of tea.

'That's right!' Fey beamed.

Thinking of tea reminded Becky of the kitchen. 'So what's with the Eiffel Tower?'

'Oh, that. Well, the shootings, of course.'

Becky held her gaze. Carmela had once told her that was important, not to let your poker opponent see your uncertainty. Well, she wasn't going to let on to Fey she didn't know –

Abruptly, she remembered the previous year's terrorist attacks in Paris. 'Yes. That was horrible.'

Fey nodded, silent for a few moments. The Romanian girls were still, too.

Along with most of her friends, Becky had tinted her profile picture with the stripes of the Tricolour. Had she tweeted *Je suis Paris*? Probably. But other than that...

'You also vowed to take on the big food producers and hold them accountable for fake ingredients, palm oil, and pesticides.' Fey was businesslike again.

'The vegetables?' Becky phrased it as a question, but she knew she was right. She was catching on, if nothing else. But she didn't remember any kidnaps, shootings, or scandals involving a woman called Fey. 'So who are you?'

Fey shrugged. 'I'm not important.' But she was studying Becky's single left shoe with interest.

Embarrassed, although why, with a flat full of schoolgirls, French monuments, and predatory felines, she should care about wardrobe eccentricities, Becky removed it. As she straightened, she noticed again how stylish Fey's patent pumps were.

'That's it!' she announced, pleased to recall at least one hot news item from the previous twelve months. 'You were sacked! For not wearing high heels.' She remembered now: a legal firm in the City had sent Fey home when she declined to wear teetering shoes for a nine hour stint at the reception desk. Becky's online community had gorged themselves on satirical outrage, much of it featuring Photoshopped images of men in stilettos.

Fey inclined her head. 'I'm flattered you remember,' she said drily, and removed her beautiful footwear. 'You must catch me up on your feminist activism since then.'

Becky flushed. Could Fey possibly know about Martin's advice earlier that week, that she might be a more obvious choice for promotion if she dressed more appealingly? She wished, now, she'd told him where to stick his favourite pencil. 'All right,' she said, head lowered. 'I can see I haven't exactly... er... followed through.'

'Your heart's in the right place,' Fey said. 'But your energy is wasted if you won't stick to one thought for more than a few minutes.'

'And you're here to punish me with a lion, a French tower, and more than enough girls to form a netball team?'

'Not punish you.' Fey stretched and stood up. 'Just... nudge you a bit.'

Becky shrank back further, being careful not to invade the space of the gangly schoolgirl next to her.

'But first things first.' Fey nodded to the gangly girl. 'We'll make everyone a nice cup of tea, and then we'll see. You sit there for a bit. After all, you've had quite a shock.'

Mouth dry, Becky allowed her spine to curve into the cushions of the sofa. Maybe Fey could do something with all those vegetables and concoct dinner for everyone. Maybe Cedric would be okay with beans on toast. Maybe, tomorrow, she'd find out if there was a long-distance bus service to Bucharest.

Maybe, if she rested her eyes for a moment, she'd feel better.

~~~

The front door closed with a thud.

'Why are you here in the dark? Are you okay?'

Becky sat up, blinking, to find her flatmate standing over her, jangling her keys.

Carmela didn't wait for an answer, already moving towards the kitchen, leaving Becky to look around the entirely empty living room. Beside her, on the floor, was one left shoe. But no sign of any patent heels.

'I'm making hot chocolate. Want one?' Yet another question that appeared to need no response.

Becky waited for the squawk when Carmela tumbled over the Eiffel Tower, but none came. Wincing, she unfolded herself from the sofa, clambered to her feet, and went to the kitchen. Peeking around the corner, she found it empty save for her Spanish friend, busy with the microwave. Its LED clock said it was just after midnight.

In silence, Becky turned again, this time to the bathroom door. She waited two, three seconds, then, with one finger, pushed it open.

The room was entirely empty, the bath dry as a bone. Becky's fluffy cream towel hung, pristine, on the rail. She reached for it, fingering it carefully, then pressed the soft fibres to her face.

'How was your day?' The flat was small enough that Carmela could call from the kitchen and be sure that Becky would hear.

'Oh... fine.' Becky straightened the towel, satisfied she'd merely fallen asleep on the sofa and had a dystopian dream. With a last look around the bathroom, she switched off the light, ignoring the faint scent of chamomile in the air.

'And you?' Becky said, as she arrived next to Carmela in the kitchen. 'Did you win?'

Carmela unwrapped the luxurious dark chocolate she only bought when she'd had a lucrative poker night. 'He didn't stand a chance.' She smiled. 'Too distracted, no attention span. People need to realise how dangerous that is.'

'Right,' said Becky, and opened the fridge in search of milk.

As she closed it, the jolt from the door caused a slight vibration in the adjacent counter. It was just enough to nudge the aubergine that was lying there into motion.

Unnoticed by either of the flatmates, it rolled gently from side to side.

Seating for Singles

I travel a lot for business.

Far from being tedious, I find the plane is an excellent hunting ground. For men, I mean.

After all, you can learn so much about someone during the cramped, dull conditions of a longhaul flight. I look for wedding rings, of course. That's a rule I don't break, unlike some. But even so, now they've done away with the smoking section (thank goodness), it would be so helpful if the airlines could seat people by relationship status. Seating for singles would make my life so much easier. In fact, I must pop that one in the suggestion box.

For example, if a man looks promising but tilts his seat back as soon as the seatbelt sign goes out, it's likely he's inconsiderate. If his nose is in his laptop for the whole flight, there's a danger he's a workaholic.

When he takes his shoes off, do his feet stink? Does he guzzle too much wine? Does he snore during his nap? Does he tackle the meal with disdain, or enthusiasm? If he leaves most of it, he could be the fussy type. Or if he does eat it, and the result is scattered debris, he might well be messy to live with. Or does he take time to fit it all back on the tray, like a Tetris puzzle? That could be a warning of OCD tendencies. Either that, or he's a software engineer. Does he look sexy and rumpled with a day's beard growth... or just rumpled?

Yes: an overnight flight is such an intimate environment, you can deduce as much about an IFB – that's Inflight Boyfriend – while crossing the Atlantic, as you would in a month's worth of dates. My peripheral vision is as sharp as an owl's.

Call me picky, but I'll only consider a guy if he waits for me to make the first move. Just because I'm up here and wearing lipstick doesn't mean I'm easy. And even when I start flirting, any inappropriate questions – like have I joined the Mile High Club, or where precisely I'm staying, for example – and I shut them down cold.

If I'm really lucky, something untoward happens, which is priceless information for how he'd respond in a crisis. For example, en route to Dubai, I was chatting happily with a witty graphic designer when the kid next to him threw up. Charisma turned instantly to sulks and I knew it was time to move on.

And I'll never forget the gorgeous hunk – Houston, I like to call him, as that's where we were heading – whom I fancied the moment he shrugged off his jacket to reveal perfectly toned arms and a tattoo of a kingfisher, my favourite bird. Unfortunately we hit turbulence mid-Atlantic and Houston screamed like a girl. So that was the end of that.

Then there was John. The signs were so auspicious: a business class seat and he was reading the *Financial Times*. He drank in moderation, and reacted well when an elderly passenger stumbled and stepped on his foot. We went out for three months and it was looking rosy, until he accepted a job in Shanghai without consulting me. Still, it'll be nice to know someone in China.

But I digress.

This chap in 12C, he looks promising. A serious-looking novel, nothing too gory. The vegetarian meal implies he's either health-conscious or an animal lover, both fine with me.

My onboard smile is never far away. 'Looks like you have business in New York,' I say. A reasonable guess from his suit trousers, blue shirt, and loosened tie. That, and the fact the plane is heading for JFK.

'Yes.' He smiles, a little wearily. 'Again.'

'I love the Big Apple,' I say. 'It energises me.'

He closes his book. 'Perhaps I'm missing its finer points.'

Bingo.

By the time we're on final approach I have his phone number, which he assures me will work as well in Manhattan as in Maidenhead. I don't like to give out my contact information, much better this way.

'I'll give you a ring tonight,' I say, calculating I'll have time for a nap beforehand. 'Now sorry, I have a few things I need to do before we land.'

'Of course.' He dutifully stows his belongings: another good sign, not a rebel.

I don't see him again until just before he disembarks, when he gives me a cheery wink. 'Looking forward to it,' he says, laptop bag slung over one shoulder as he trudges with the others up the jetty.

My friend Patty, also stationed at the main door to bid farewell to our passengers, overhears. 'I don't believe you.' She rolls her eyes. 'You're going to get into trouble one of these days.'

'There's no policy against it,' I reply. I'm not stupid, I checked the crew handbook. 'Anyway, you can't talk about being overfamiliar.' Patty transferred to us from American Airlines and became a laughing stock when she failed to recognise Earl Spencer in first class one day. 'You blundered in and asked Princess Diana's brother if you could call him Chuck.'

~ ~ ~

On the crew bus to our hotel, Patty says, 'I assume you have plans for tonight?'

'Yep,' I say cheerfully. 'With 12C.'

'Good luck,' she says, yawning. 'Hope he's the one.'

I smile. I hope so too, but it doesn't matter much if he's not. I also have business cards from 18A, 9F, and 25D.

After all, there are plenty more fish in the sky.

Hikers' Hut

She'd been insane to agree to a Swiss walking weekend with her new man. She'd pictured lakefront strolls and chocolate truffles; he'd packed a map, compass, and ice axe.

The cloud descended an hour ago. Her ankle was twisted, her fingers turned numb. She couldn't keep up and they were barely speaking.

Six paces ahead, he stopped abruptly and pointed to a yellow sign: *Kistenpasshütte 30 min.*

'It won't be much – a roof, a bunk. A blanket, if we're lucky.'

A hikers' hut? Up here, where even the cowbells had fallen silent? Relief flooded her.

She took his hand.

~ ~ ~

Author's note: Originally published at julievalerie.com.

Traffic Lights

Sometimes I talk to traffic lights.

I asked my hairdresser if she thought that meant I was nuts, and she said, 'Only if they answer back.'

I changed the topic after that.

The traffic signals in question were a few hundred yards from my office, on a steep stretch of dual carriageway with a 50mph limit. It's the kind of incline you barely notice in a car: a gentle roll through the green landscape of Norfolk. But on a bike, the hill was a different matter. It became a long, slow grind where my pedals seemed to turn slower and slower, where I had to look down at the tarmac road to confirm I was still moving. I made this climb every morning, the final hurdle on my six mile journey, because Malcolm insisted we couldn't afford two cars, not when he was ploughing every last penny into his environmental consultancy firm. He specialised in wind farms, which struck me as especially ironic every time a gust hit me in the face. Malcolm, meanwhile, drove to Norwich each day in a sleek maroon Audi, which he said was important to create the right image with clients. The car was leased, of course, but was a luxury model, with a sunroof and heated leather seats. I comforted myself that my bicycle did, indeed, have a sunroof – and a rain roof, and a sleet roof, and sometimes a snow roof. But a heated saddle on those January and February mornings would have been awfully welcome.

'Anyway,' I said, on the most recent occasion we argued about money, 'if you really want to create a green impression, you should ride the bloody bike, not me.'

'Don't be ridiculous,' he said, which I'd noticed was becoming his standard answer to everything I uttered, regardless of whether it was a complaint, suggestion, or observation about the weather. In fact, I couldn't remember the last time he found an opinion of mine valuable.

The office at the end of my pedalling was a company which rents out construction equipment, and I'd been a bookkeeper there for seven years. We had over two hundred different items available, including a range of portable toilets. I'm pretty sure Malcolm was embarrassed by my employer. For a long time he nagged me to look for something better, more prestigious. Gradually, though, he lost interest and simply referred to my job, when we were among friends, as *loo keeping.* Then he stopped referring to it at all. But since Friday night dinners with friends had dwindled too, it hardly mattered.

Malcolm, on the other hand, ate out frequently. When I frowned over his credit card bill and wondered what I could cut from our Sainsbury's grocery list to ease the pinch, he'd explain he was wooing potential clients.

'And you're so scatty about keeping receipts,' I scolded, trying desperately to keep his records in order, in case the Inland Revenue got curious. 'Half of these dinners are missing.'

'I'm building a business, Esther,' he replied. 'I haven't got time for bean counting.'

'Well, bean counting's what I do all day,' I said, raising my chin and preparing to defend my job. 'Maybe you should employ me.'

Sure enough, 'Don't be ridiculous,' came the immediate answer.

He could, however, afford a secretary – or Environmental Intern, as he preferred to call Melanie. She was around fifteen years younger than Malcolm, studying for a Masters in something impressively green sounding. She had swirly designs on her fingernails, and freckles dotting a little snub nose. The freckles ran up her forearms too, and beyond, I expect. When I called his office, she sometimes answered the phone in a cheery, upbeat voice which lowered when she heard it was me. Other times I called, nobody answered at all.

'If you haven't got the receipt,' I said, exasperated because I wanted to soak my saddle-sore limbs in a hot sudsy bath, not untangle his ghastly finances, 'at least make a note of who was at the dinner.'

He looked at me blankly, then reached for the television remote. 'Four of us,' he said, turning up the volume for the news. 'The guys from VentoTech, I think.'

But I was good at my job: it was the receipts which eventually made me suspicious. The evening I'd walked the last two miles home because of a puncture in my rear tyre, to find the house cold and unlit, I spotted the pattern. The missing receipts were all from the same three establishments: two restaurants, and a hotel.

I mended the puncture, listening carefully for the place where the air hissed out of the inner tube in the same way the last oxygen was hissing out of my marriage. Then I checked the restaurant menus: the amounts on the credit card statement were barely enough to feed four men dinner. But two people? Two could have dined very well indeed. As for the hotel, yes, it had a restaurant. It was perfectly possible Malcolm had taken clients to the dining room there. But the amounts were high, often a round number, in the way a meal doesn't tend to be. A room, however, is a different matter.

I kept quiet, biding my time, struggling up that hill on my bike each morning, and watching my meagre salary plop into our joint bank account before ebbing away on one business expense after another.

Then came the conference, on environmental subsidies, in Bournemouth. I said nothing. I smiled, I shrugged, I wished him a pleasant trip as I hopped on my bike early one February morning. But six miles in the chilly mist gave me plenty of time to simmer. I added up the number of miles I'd pedalled since Malcolm started his business. I calculated the number of days I'd made the right turn at the traffic lights on the steep hill, gripping my handlebars tightly as cars and lorries sped past, so close my bike shook.

That's how it started, you see: talking to the traffic lights. Having panted up that hill, it was so lovely if the lights switched to green at just the right second, so I didn't lose what little momentum I'd built. If they changed for me, I began to thank them. I knew it was silly, but over time I convinced myself the lights were turning more often in my favour, sometimes even going green immediately after they'd turned red for my lane. With a job chasing payments for mobile toilets, and my marriage actually going down the toilet, I needed to believe in something.

So, with Malcolm in Bournemouth, I rode my bike dutifully on Tuesday and Wednesday. I considered taking a taxi, to spite him, but by now, with years of biking behind me, I could feel the power in my legs. Power, and possibility.

On Thursday, I phoned the conference hotel and asked to be put through to his room. I wasn't all that surprised when a cheery, upbeat voice answered.

A month went by, a bitter, sullen month when Malcolm tried to tell me I was being ridiculous, but he must have known how pathetic that sounded. And he knew, too, how much he had to lose: the house was in our joint names, but a cottage in Yorkshire, left to me by my father, was in my name alone. The only assets belonging solely to Malcolm were a leased car and a life insurance policy.

Eventually, he suggested marriage counselling and I agreed, if only to buy time. I wasn't planning to stay with him; I just needed to arrange my alternative.

So that's why, one rainy April day, I didn't ride my bike to work.

'I'll pick you up later,' he said. 'We can go to the counsellor together.'

'I can bike,' I said, thinking I didn't want to travel anywhere with him. Not any more.

'No,' he insisted. 'It looks bad, you showing up on that rattly thing.'

I raised my eyebrows. Didn't he see that it was a bit late to worry about appearances? He'd been betraying me with his assistant, using my salary to do it, and he was concerned with transport arrangements?

Still, I went along with it. 'Okay,' I said. 'I'll be ready at four.'

So there I was, waiting out of sight under a tree near the main road, sheltering from the drizzle and watching the spray kicked up by the cars speeding by on the dual carriageway. I saw the maroon Audi come up the hill from town and join the right turn lane, Malcolm naturally assuming I'd be loitering outside my office. Just then the signal turned amber, then red, and the Audi stopped obediently. I stared at the lights, a slight smile on my lips. But my gaze was implacable and my eyes glittered. Almost immediately, the right turn signal changed back to green. So too did the light for the traffic hurtling down the hill, the oncoming lorry no doubt roaring along at 50mph or even a bit more on the wet road. Nonetheless, the Audi trusted the traffic light and made the turn, steering without question, right into the path of the truck.

~ ~ ~

Everyone was so kind. Their platitudes in the subsequent days swirled around me.

'Such a shock,' they murmured, and I nodded.

'He didn't stand a chance,' they offered, and I agreed.

'At least you'll be comfortably off,' they said awkwardly, once the life insurance payout was confirmed.

I dipped my head delicately and said nothing.

Sometimes, I talk to traffic lights.

~ ~ ~

Author's note: Once a week, I ride my bike to work before dawn. The journey includes a final, tedious hill, and I distract myself by pondering stories. When I found myself thanking the traffic signals at the top of the climb, this plot was born.

The Sandwich Shop

'Do you think duck goes better with cream cheese or pickled onions?' I ask.

'You what?' Stephen looks up from his computer.

'Anton, at the sandwich shop. He said if I guess his favourite filling, he'll get me a date with Claude.'

'Oh, really?' Stephen's face is impassive, his attention clearly on his latest spreadsheet.

'So I'm trying all the combinations. Well, most of them. Probably not prawn and fig.'

Stephen sighs. He sighs at me a lot. 'If you do try that one, don't bring it near me.'

~~~

I've been at Walden Windows for two years and on most days during that time, I've bought lunch at Anton's. His bread is by far the best in town, he's friendly, and there's a certain continental class to his shop which the other cafés here lack.

But three months ago, at the beginning of June, his nephew arrived from Nantes to help for the summer. With dark hair just long enough to be tied back, a turned up nose, and thick eyelashes, Claude was literally the dishiest thing in the shop. Ooh la la. I could barely eat my cheese and pickle baguette that day, knowing he'd baked the soft, fragrant bread.

'Anton,' I hissed, a week later, 'tell me more about Claude.'

Anton was restocking the display of crisps on the counter. 'What you want to know?'

My French friend has been in England for thirty years but hasn't lost his accent.

'How long is he here for?'

The sandwich maestro shrugged, a gesture perfected in his homeland, I expect. 'Oh, the summer, I think.'

I wondered if that meant an English summer, over by the first week of September, or the French Riviera kind, which would surely stretch into November.

'Well, like, is he, er, single?' Regardless of the length of summer, I couldn't afford to be bashful.

'Why you want to know?' Anton said, annoyingly.

'Well, duh...' I tapped a two pound coin on his glass counter to chivvy him along.

'I think so. Why, you like 'im?'

I made a face to imply it was obvious, wasn't it? Who wouldn't like the dreamy, dark-eyed Gaul?

The trouble was, I didn't get to talk much to Claude. He started work around four in the morning each day, and was mostly in the back of the shop, baking, until noon. I wasn't going to hang around to strike up conversation in the predawn hours, and despite buying my lunch later, I never managed to bump into him going home.

So, after Claude had been at the café a fortnight, I grew more bold.

'You could set us up,' I implored Anton. 'I bet he doesn't have any friends in Saffron Walden.' Being a small market town, Walden is populated either by old people, or those who commute to London for work. Walden Windows does most of our business with the latter, or their wives.

'He no right for you, Jessie.' Anton didn't look up from the huge loaf he was wrapping for the customer beside me. 'He not your dream guy.'

'How would you know?' I asked crossly. 'He absolutely is.'

Anton said nothing, just did his shrug.

'How many sandwiches do I have to buy, for a date?' I was thinking my next birthday could be a baguette party.

'Hah. I not sell my nephew,' he replied, pretending to be offended. He completed the loaf transaction, then seemed surprised I was still there, loitering with my sausage bap and can of Diet Coke. 'I tell you what, Miss Jessica.' He looked at the ceiling as if wondering why I had been sent to try his patience. 'The day you order my favourite filling, I fix you up with your dream guy.'

'Deal!' I said, before I really thought about it. How hard could it be to work my way through the menu of fillings? I'd even eat avocado, if I had to.

Deep in thought, I walked the short distance back to Walden Windows, where I was irritated to find a woman browsing our showroom. She looked well-heeled, usually a good sign, but I was keen to devour my lunch and then make a plan for deducing Anton's favourite filling. As patiently as I could, I explained the options for casement styles and recommended she consider the style of her home to help her decide. Then I gave her a stack of brochures and, with my best smile, opened the door. With the shop to myself again, I retreated to the back office.

Stephen was bent over the printer, pulling out the inky paper remnants which usually accompany a jam. He does our accounts, billing and ordering, and, reluctantly, our computer support. Our boss, Clifford, spends most of his time out selling to clients or supervising the two installation crews. So it's usually just Stephen and me. He's nice enough, but on the nerdy side, with glasses that don't quite fit. Ugly shoes, too: I don't think I've seen him wear anything but battered trainers.

Unlike the last office I worked, where the girls formed a close bond over dating dilemmas, Stephen appears either bored or dismissive of my love life. Last year, after the chap from a car dealership stood me up on a chilly Thursday night, all Stephen had to say was, 'Told you so.'

And in February, when I was thrilled to reach a fourth date with a trainee dentist right before Valentine's Day, Stephen caught me crying over being dumped by text message. 'Not worth it,' was the verdict that time. In short, he's never been the least bit supportive, especially not the day I tried to get ready at the office so I could hop on the 5:38 to Bishop's Stortford to meet the son of a customer.

'Do you think that's ethical?' Stephen had said, after demanding to know why I'd been in the small office toilet for twenty-five minutes. 'Going out with a client?'

'He's not a client,' I protested, deliberating between a red crew neck and a black blouse. 'Anyway, we sell windows. It's not like I'm his doctor or something.'

Stephen said nothing, just glowered.

'Well?' I prompted, jiggling the clothing but still blocking him from using the loo. 'Which?'

He sniffed. 'The red. You look nice in red.'

'Thank you!' I called, as I locked the door again. 'See, you can be helpful, if you try!'

~~~

Now, my phone rings, a customer who's due for installation later this month, wanting to know what happens in the event of bad weather.

'We work around it, Mrs Ford,' I say, as reassuringly as I can. 'No, no, we won't leave you overnight with holes in your walls.'

But the truth is, things can get awkward if it pours for days, like it did last autumn. The fitters get restless, customers become anxious, and Stephen tuts about cash flow.

I put the phone down. 'She's tizzing about crappy weather.'

'Could happen,' Stephen says, not looking up. 'Autumn and all.'

I sigh. 'I can't believe we're in September already!' I have the worst foreboding that Claude might return to France soon. 'And I haven't guessed Anton's bloody favourite!'

'For heaven's sake.' Stephen's unusually snappish. 'Not that stupid sandwich thing, still.'

I inspect today's filling – tuna and beetroot – morosely. 'I didn't realise there were so many permutations. I'm losing track of what I've tried.'

'You need a spreadsheet,' Stephen huffs, looking half interested now he knows he can make one of his beloved Excel tables. 'And it's not a permutation, it's a combination.'

I don't ask for clarification. I'm actually not bad at maths, but with Stephen around, I pretend to hate numbers. That way I don't get stuck covering his work when he goes hiking in the Brecon Beacons.

I bite into my sandwich, still glum. 'I'm going to die an old maid,' I proclaim, which is a bit over the top considering I'm thirty-two.

Stephen gives me a sidelong look. 'You could try being more open-minded.'

'What's that supposed to mean? I *am* open-minded.' I think back to this year's Cambridge Folk Festival and some of the frankly unbelievable sights there.

'About the guys you go out with. It's like you have a list of requirements. They have to be handsome, rich, sexy, aloof, fashionable, and preferably foreign. Ideally, arrogant chauvinists too.'

This is the most Stephen's ever said to me at one time.

'I didn't realise you were paying attention,' I reply snarkily.

He just shrugs, silent again now.

'Anyway,' I say, stung, 'the dentist had bad dress sense. And the hunk from Bishop's Stortford wasn't foreign.'

'Forget it,' says Stephen.

But twenty minutes later, he emails me a spreadsheet. I click on the attachment and find it's called Sandwich Tracker.

~ ~ ~

By mid-September, the weather has indeed turned foul. I'm standing in Anton's shop one soggy Tuesday, listening to the rain plopping into the puddles outside.

'It's no good,' I say, staring forlornly down at my printed spreadsheet. 'I think I've tried everything. I don't think you have a favourite, do you? I bet you go home and eat, what, quiche every night?'

Anton laughs. 'Your sheet is very sweet, Jessica.'

'Stephen made it for me,' I reply. 'But I don't think it's working. You promised me a date but I'm no closer, am I?'

Anton stops and leans his forearms on the counter. 'Don't be glum,' he says. 'Of course you are close.'

'I've tried chicken and apricot, and ham and Roquefort, and egg and cress, and beef and horseradish.' I run my finger along the columns. 'I've even tried weird ones, like pineapple and smoked trout.'

'You don't trust Stephen?' Anton asks now, peering at my sheet upside down. 'He is good guy. He help you, yes?'

'Oh, I don't know. He's never enthusiastic about my dates,' I say, tapping my fingers on the sheet. 'Maybe I'll just have chicken mayo today, Anton.'

Anton nods. 'If that's what you want.'

I sniff, not trying to hide my frustration. 'Well, I don't have any other options left, do I?'

Anton raises his eyebrows at me, then jerks his head to the sheet. 'Sure of that, Jessie?'

Then I see it, the one empty box. I missed it before, because the tick marks from two neighbouring squares were infringing on the space. I trace the row, then the column.

'Roast beef and Brie,' I announce, as the door opens behind me and another customer comes into the shop. 'I'll have beef and Brie, please.'

Anton has a baguette in one hand, ready to slice. He stops, beaming. 'Ah! My favourite!'

'Really?' My heart lurches as I wait to see if he's kidding.

His eyes twinkle as he lifts the serrated knife.

'Really?' I say again. 'I've got it? Your favourite?' Suddenly, I can't stand still. 'So you'll get me a date?'

'What's up?' from behind me, Stephen steps forward.

'*Voilà!*' Anton beams and apparently forgets about assembling my sandwich. 'She did it,' he tells Stephen, who darts a look at me. 'Jessie has guessed, so she gets her date, *non?*'

Stephen goes slightly pink, but I barely notice.

'When?' I ask Anton, a shiver zinging through me.

'When would you like to take her out?'

Why is Anton talking to Stephen?

'Er, how's Saturday?'

And why is Stephen talking to me?

'Hang on a minute,' I say. 'Anton, you're going to set me up with Claude, right?'

'*Non.*' Back with the sandwich making, he waggles a slice of roast beef. 'With Stephen. He is your – how you say – your dreamy guy.'

I look at Stephen, whose cheeks are definitely red now. But he stands his ground. 'Saturday okay for you, Jess?'

'Look, sorry, there's been some mistake,' I stall. 'Anton...' I crane my neck, trying to see if Claude is in the kitchen, hoping he'll come sauntering out right now and sweep me off for a picnic under the bandstand.

'No mistake,' Anton says cheerily. '*Non.* I am sure.' He holds up a wedge of Brie and sniffs it. '*Bien,*' he says. 'I shall make another of these, for myself.'

'Forget the sandwich, Anton.' My voice rises in pitch. 'My date –'

'*Oui,*' he says. 'Your date is with Stephen, who has helped you with the sandwich challenge.'

'Yes, but –'

'He is much better for you than Claude.'

'Sorry? I don't understand.'

'*Oui,* you are much more... how you say... compatible.' Anton nods definitively. 'You know nothing about Claude, Jessie.'

'I do!' I take a breath to continue, but Anton is too quick.

'You no know how he votes. You no know if he want kids. You no know if he wants his wife to work or stay home. You no know if he's kind to his grandmother. You no know if he keeps a kitten or a *tarentule* as a pet.'

'So?' I lift my chin. Claude's hot. I can take my chances on that other stuff. Although I admit I'd prefer the fluffy feline over the nasty spider.

Anton jerks his head at Stephen. 'What we know about Stephen? We know he help you at work and with your love life.'

'He doesn't,' I protest. 'The second one, I mean.'

'I would if you'd let me.' Stephen's been watching quietly but now he speaks. 'And Anton's right, you do know me better.'

Anton chimes in, nodding at my office mate. 'How many kids he want?'

'Lots,' I say, without thinking.

Anton looks to Stephen for confirmation and gets a nod and a shrug. 'Eventually, obviously.'

'What did he buy his *maman* for her birthday?'

'I've no idea,' I blurt, then relent. 'A digital camera. I only know that because she phoned him at work, for help with it.'

'Does he vote the same way as you? Does he give the blood? Does he like *Strictly Come Dancing*?' Anton is like a prosecuting barrister now, not a sandwich pusher.

I fold my arms. 'This is ridiculous.'

Stephen, though, looks intrigued. 'Wait, it's kind of fun. Come on, Jessie, do I?'

I shake my head, before snapping, 'Mostly, sometimes, no. Now, Anton, stop it.'

Anton wipes his hands on his apron before turning and pulling the door to the kitchen closed. Then he comes around the counter, moving heavily. 'Listen to me, Jessica. Claude, he is a good baker, but, how you say... a bit of a chauvinist pig.'

I say nothing but purse my lips.

'He no visit his grandmother, not even on her deathbed. He more interested in motorbikes. He takes girls out once, twice, no more. He is... a heart taker.'

'Breaker.' Stephen corrects him, then gives me a look.

'But –' I want to say, every girl likes a challenge, right?

'You waste your time with him, I promise.' Anton puts a hand on my arm and turns me gently towards Stephen.

'Your Stephen, he knows you better, you know him better. He is good lad, he treat you nice, Jessie. He is your dream guy.'

Well, this is awkward. I don't want to hurt my colleague's feelings, but this wasn't my plan at all.

'Jess, I'd like to take you out for dinner,' Stephen says now. 'Get to know you more.'

I sniff. 'According to Anton, you already know me just fine.'

'A little, yes,' Stephen replies. 'And I agree with Anton... I think we could be a match.'

I've never seen him so assertive. Still, I glance wistfully at the kitchen door.

'Margaritas?' Stephen suggests, holding my gaze. 'Followed by Thai? Then dancing, and ice cream on the way home?'

Hmm, maybe he does have an idea of what an ideal date involves.

'Okay,' I say slowly. 'On one condition. I'll go out with you if...' I look around the shop, searching for inspiration, something to test him.

Stephen waits, head tilted, while Anton is already beaming.

'I'll go out with you if you can name my favourite sandwich.' I brandish the spreadsheet, as if it's evidence of the impossible task.

But Stephen laughs. 'Anton, I think she likes me after all.'

'Why?' I demand, thinking, it's not that easy, is it?

'Sausage and chutney,' Stephen rattles off, 'with mature cheddar. Preferably with thinly sliced cucumber, but lettuce will do if not. On a bloomer bap, cut into four pieces, not two. Granny Smith apple and a can of Diet Coke on the side. Half a Twix to finish.'

Anton lets out a belly laugh which could wake Claude's dead grandmother all the way in the Loire.

'Stephen is the winner!' he declares, slapping him jovially on the arm.

'Shall we get back?' Stephen plucks my beef and Brie lunch off the counter and gives Anton a conspiratorial smile. Then he opens the door of the sandwich shop and waves me through.

I incline my head gracefully, determined to remain a little aloof. But as we dodge the puddles on the way back to Walden Windows, I think about Anton's parting words and I'm not sure I agree.

I think, just maybe, the winner in this sandwich saga might be me.

Christmas House

It appeared every Christmas Eve, and was gone by Boxing Day. On the mantel stood a perfect miniature house, carved from wood, mere inches high.

But lights twinkled from inside. And leaning close, she could hear laughter, voices, merriment. A family.

'No touching,' warned Grandpa. 'The leprechauns won't like it.'

Her grandfather worked tirelessly, but their stockings never bulged. The roast bird was perpetually scrawny and the table set for only three.

'You know it was just a candle in there,' says her brother, years later.

She nods, but her eyes are on the mantel.

Because tomorrow is Christmas Eve.

~~~

Author's note: Originally published at julievalerie.com.

Travels with a Persian Rug

Only a complete lunatic would try to fly somewhere the Sunday after Thanksgiving. And yet, there we were, O'Hare Airport, Sami battling to steer our absurd luggage cart through the shuffling crowds.

Everyone looked miserable. Half had basked in the pumpkin pie-scented warmth of their familial circle, and didn't want to return home. The other half had endured prickling awkwardness with either their own kin, or, as in my case, the in-laws, and were now being further tortured in a seething herd of fellow travellers.

I could have helped Sami with the cart but I was determined not to be obliging. I hadn't wanted to go to Chicago for Thanksgiving, pleading to see my own family and sister in Santa Barbara instead.

'But you can go at Christmas,' Sami had said. He didn't want to visit his maniacal father either, but after four years of us ducking and dodging, Jafar was threatening to come to us in Seattle.

'Michelle won't be there at Christmas. Andrew's parents are taking them on a Disney cruise.'

I had met my baby nephew only once, had fallen shockingly in love, and was aching to see little Danny again. He smelled of warm cookies and had clung to my finger like a climber in a crevasse. What's more, I was dying to escape the rain and enjoy Thanksgiving lunch on the terrace of my parents' graceful white house with its Spanish tiled roof. Chicago's sleet and bitter wind held no allure for me.

I was even less in need of a dose of Sami's Iranian father. Ironically, his heritage had been part of the attraction when we had met, twelve years ago now, in a quirky café in downtown Berkeley. I had been mesmerised by Sami's molten chocolate eyes and thick dark hair. As I got to know him, I discovered with delight that his American mother had instilled western values in her son: he was fully supportive of my ambitions to specialise in genetics counselling. To me, he was an exotic, modern-day romantic hero.

The magic wore thin when we moved to Seattle after graduation, so that Sami could take a lucrative job in software. The rain had tarnished the sheen on our marriage as my career sputtered and stalled. I found myself stuck in a doctor's office, typing, filing, and greeting. Sami's luminous smile made fewer appearances these days.

Finally, we reached the special security desk. Our cargo, a Persian rug, was too large to go through the regular baggage system.

'What the hell was he thinking?' I snarled to Sami for about the tenth time. 'What a damn crazy thing to do.'

'He meant well. It's his culture to give us stuff.'

'We should have gotten rid of it.'

Unfortunately, Jafar had given both us and the rug a ride to the airport, double kissing us goodbye at the kerbside with tears in his eyes.

'C'mon, Tess, we can't just dump a large package in the check-in hall.'

'And it's going to cost a fortune. I know it.' I prided myself on travelling light and had arrived in Chicago with only handbaggage.

'I'll pay,' Sami said curtly. Money was another thing we had started to bicker about.

Jafar's previous presents had usually missed the mark, but this one was bordering on ridiculous.

'I have for you a gift,' he had announced proudly after lunch on Thursday. Instead of turkey and pecan pie, we had feasted on saffron-coloured shrimp stir-fry. To my dismay, Jafar's Iranian second wife had eaten in the kitchen, refusing my polite urging to join us.

Our gift was a mammoth green plastic package, the size of a nightstand. It took two people to lift.

'This is coming all the way from Iran,' Jafar said. He pronounced the country Ee-rrahn. 'It is an antique carpet.'

I went pale. My nerves were already stretched from the effort of being polite to my father-in-law. He was an impetuous man, given to grand gestures and appallingly sexist comments. I knew his attitudes were cultural, but he was living in America now, for heaven's sake. On previous occasions, he had asked me if I knew how to drive, whether I worked, and if I exercised my right to vote. The implication was that his son's wife should be doing none of these things.

In the early days, Sami had defended me and womankind vigorously, insisting I was a better driver than he and that of course I worked. He'd even thrown in for good measure that I could run a mile faster than most men. On this visit, though, when Jafar trotted out derisive remarks, Sami had sighed and kept his eyes fixed on the European soccer on television. He doesn't even like soccer.

We'd gathered around the monstrous package.

'Do not open it,' Jafar ordered. 'It is sealed, for you to take home.'

Great, I thought. We now have to navigate an airport on the busiest day of the year with a massive, unknown parcel given to us by an Iranian national. We would probably get body searched.

I looked at Sami, willing him to decline the gift.

He too was pondering the rug doubtfully, but he wouldn't meet my eyes. He knew how particular – fussy – I am about our home. Nothing gets in to our neat townhouse without my approval, and most of what does is rejected within a couple of years, as my tastes evolve. More often than not, gifts from stylish girlfriends are hidden in closets. The free mugs that Sami tries to bring back from computing conferences are donated within days. So there was no way on earth I was going to live with a hideous Persian artefact.

Despite my glare, Sami thanked his father and they hugged awkwardly.

'What colour is it?' I asked, swallowing the acid in my throat and summoning my manners.

Jafar looked uncertain. 'Red,' he said, after a pause.

'Milky,' his timid wife offered simultaneously, stretching her minimal English to its limit.

They didn't know, of course. They'd never actually seen the rug. Jafar had probably ordered it by telephone, talking rapidly across nine time zones to the friend of a friend. I shook my head in frustration. Coincidentally, I had been thinking about buying a rug for our dining area, but this sure as heck wasn't it. It was undoubtedly valuable and I could only imagine what it had cost to ship from Tehran. Why couldn't he have just given us the money, and I would have gone to Pottery Barn and picked out something tasteful?

Seven hours later, we were home, exhausted, barely talking. I hadn't slept well for four nights, resentment and a sagging air mattress conspiring against sweet dreams.

To my surprise, the excess baggage had cost a mere forty dollars. And the X-ray machine had revealed nothing sinister lurking within. I had entertained a brief fantasy that American Airlines might misplace it, but of course it had shown up with brash defiance in the luggage hall at Tacoma.

Sami was out of breath from hauling the green plastic interloper up the stairs from our garage. 'We can put it into storage,' he said.

He knew he was in big trouble. His lovechild would probably have received a warmer welcome in our home. Meanwhile, though, I had made espresso in my beloved De'Longhi machine and was inhaling the comforting steam. And I had to admit, I was curious.

I kicked off my shoes and shrugged. 'We may as well take a look.'

Sami slit the plastic and the carpet came popping out, like the dough in a can of ready-to-bake crescent rolls. Together, we wriggled and pulled until the rug flopped onto the dark hardwood floor.

I folded my arms and prepared to hate it. 'This must be the back, right?'

The colours were too muted, too calm. But no, closer inspection revealed this was the front of the rug: taupe and cream, with smoky blue-grey hints and a little sage. Jafar's wife had been correct with *milky*. The pattern, of course, was swirly, traditional, uninspiring. However, the rug was a good size, huge, in fact. It might even be big enough to accommodate our sleek Ethan Allen dining table.

I walked to the far side of the room, looking at the rug from a distance. I tilted my head, pursed my lips, narrowed my eyes.

Sami was watching me, his body tense.

I sniffed. 'It might just work.'

'Where?' he asked.

I didn't answer, already moving the dining room chairs.

Between us, we lifted the table, struggled to move it, dragged the heavy rug into position, and put the table back. As I suspected, there was still ample room for the chairs.

I stood back, hands on hips, ignoring the twinge in my lower back. How, exactly, was this possible? The taupe in the rug coordinated perfectly with the Benjamin

Moore paint on our walls. The cream echoed the silk of the drapes, and the gentle smoky blue enhanced my large glossy lamps, which had been a luxurious splurge last birthday. The traditional style was a punchy contrast to the modern lines of the table and the striped covers on our custom dining chairs. It was as if it had been chosen for this space and no other.

I reached out an experimental toe and found the rug was densely woven, yet disarmingly soft. I got down on my hands and knees and sniffed: wool, of course, a little cinnamon, nothing too offensive. I circled the table, looking from every angle, went into the kitchen, viewed it from there. I was a mother sheep, deciding whether to accept an orphaned lamb as my own.

Sami stood to one side, eyebrows raised, knowing better than to interrupt.

I flicked the switch on the coffee machine again. 'It can stay.'

'Really?' He was surprised.

I nodded. 'It looks pretty good.'

Actually, it looked perfect. I flushed and dropped my eyes to the rug.

Carefully, as if he might get clawed at any moment, Sami put his arms around me. I stiffened but then relaxed, letting my cheek fall against his chest. He was wearing the cashmere sweater I'd bought him last Christmas.

'Okay?' He kissed my forehead.

'Yeah.' I exhaled slowly. 'Sorry I was moody all weekend.'

'You were great,' he said, and we both knew he was lying.

After a pause, Sami spoke. 'How about we call in sick tomorrow and go get a Christmas tree?'

I blinked, opening my mouth to snap that I couldn't possibly. The medical practice would be besieged by patients who had burned themselves making sweet potato casserole, or cut themselves carving turkey. Or – and these were the worst kind – those who had decided they couldn't face December without upping their dose of Prozac.

Still, I looked again at our Persian rug. I had been so wrong about that. I lifted my head and looked into my husband's chocolate eyes.

'You choose it,' he said. 'I'll chop.'

Something in his gaze told me he was asking a bigger question.

'A tree?' I gave a tiny nod, willing at least to meet him halfway. 'I'd love to.'

Saving Saffron Sweeting: Chapter 1

I was balanced on an eight-foot ladder with a mouth full of curtain hooks when I realised that my husband was cheating.

The individual pieces of the picture suddenly came together, making terrifying sense. I blinked hard, then stared at my knuckles, which were now white from gripping the ladder. But the image wouldn't subside. The picture I saw was James with another woman.

I was hanging curtains in my client Rebecca's bedroom, and the project was almost complete. This was great, as she'd been excited to give the room a whole new look after she'd recently come to the end of a long relationship.

'I'm ready to move on. Grace, I want a totally fresh look,' she'd told me when we met to discuss how I could help her. 'Something luxurious, maybe a little sensual. I don't plan on being single forever.'

I was still new in the design business and it was a huge deal for me not only to land a new client, but also one who had money to spend and some kind of clue what she wanted. My first few months had been a real struggle and I was starting to question my talents. Other business owners had stressed the importance of tapping my personal network to get things rolling, so James had spread the word around his office. Apparently, he had done a good job of promoting my abilities to Rebecca, his company's marketing manager. She had been great to work for and seemed appreciative of my suggestions. The only slight issue was that in the last few weeks she had been anxious to speed things up and get the bedroom completed.

Eager to please, I had been beavering away and attempting to charm my suppliers into hurrying. After getting the curtains up, I planned to hit the shops for accessories, and then the room would be ready for whatever action she had in mind.

My work had been interrupted by a knock on the front door of Rebecca's condo. I'd opened it to find a bubbly young woman, who presented me with a pair of pink stilettos.

'Oh!' she said. 'I was hoping Becca would be home. Can you let her know Kerry returned these?'

'I think she's at work,' I said, taking the shoes. 'I'm her bedroom designer.'

'Ooh, you mean the love nest? Can I see it?'

'Er, it's not finished yet,' I replied. 'I expect she'd rather show you herself.'

Kerry shrugged. 'Okay. I'll catch up with her.' She turned and was a few steps down the hall before she added, 'And tell her I want to hear all about Vegas and this James guy. He sounds delish!'

My mind was still on the curtains. I'd shut the door and put the cute shoes down, before returning to the bedroom.

Climbing back up the ladder, I thought, No wonder Rebecca wants to hurry this room. She's met some man in Las Vegas and needs her bedroom back. I was stretching to try to hook the edge of the curtain to the last ring on the pole when the dark feeling began to slither over me.

Did the ladder wobble? Had one of San Francisco's famous earthquakes nudged it? Or was the lurch, the sway, the feeling of my stomach dropping to the new wool rug, due to something else? I checked the new tear-drop chandelier hanging above the bed. As a British transplant to the Bay Area, I had spent the first couple of years diving under our dining table at the slightest tremor. But by now I had learned that if the light fixtures weren't swaying, the seismic jolt was all in my head. The glass drops of Rebecca's chandelier stared back at me steadily, not even winking, let alone dancing.

I had the presence of mind not to swallow my curtain hooks as I took a huge gulp and slid down the ladder. I slumped onto the new and naked mattress as I thought about my husband's recent conference trip to Las Vegas and how edgy he had been since. I remembered our paths crossing briefly in the kitchen, the first morning after his return.

'How was it?' I'd asked, digging through the drawer for my favourite cereal spoon.

'Okay, I guess.' He reached for the tea bags.

James seemed dispirited and I thought perhaps the industry analysts had given his company, a mobile security start-up, a tough time.

'Are you home this evening?' he wanted to know.

'Probably,' I called over my shoulder. I was already heading to my computer to check whether anyone had emailed for decor advice. Even at that hour, my mind was firmly on my fragile business.

But that day I'd been called by a potential customer to discuss her family room and, as was typical, she could only meet me in the evening. I was hard at work researching inspiration pictures when James came home, and within minutes I headed out to my appointment. After more than an hour of fruitless discussion on the merits of contemporary versus rustic style, I drove the forty minutes home across the Dumbarton Bridge to find my husband was already asleep.

With an uncomfortable feeling, I also recalled the previous evening, when he'd come home from work early and asked to talk to me, but I'd been flying out of the door to my women's networking group. This had been the pattern of life recently: we seemed to pass each other fleetingly, our schedules never lining up for longer than it took to brew a pot of tea.

And now I had learned that Rebecca had hooked up with someone called James in Las Vegas. My James had been acting oddly since he had returned from there. Keep calm, I told myself, it's probably fine.

But it wasn't fine. The third and ugly part of the truth was literally staring me in the face. Rebecca's favourite colour was purple and despite some reservations on my part, she had been adamant about using a strong shade of aubergine. We'd finally agreed on a sophisticated tan for three walls, painting the dramatic colour as an accent behind her bed. And although James usually showed precious little interest in any of my decorating ideas, we had been talking about Rebecca's project just before his trip, when we'd been in the kitchen long enough to empty the dishwasher together.

'How is your client list coming along?' he'd asked, shaking leftover water from a wine glass.

'Slowly,' I'd replied. 'Rebecca's bedroom is nearly finished but I don't have anyone lined up after her.'

He didn't say anything but had stretched over my head to put some plates away.

Happy to talk about my work, I'd let my brain run on. 'I hope it all comes together okay. That accent colour was such a bold choice.'

He'd pulled a slight face. 'Yeah, purple always reminds me of something my grandad would have had.'

I had dropped the topic, as I'd learned during our years together that James based most of his interior design dislikes on the vivid avocado and orange combinations in his grandfather's house. He thought any room featuring retro patterns or an accent wall was hideous.

Now, I leaped off the mattress as though it had bitten me on the behind. I was convinced I hadn't mentioned purple, aubergine or any other arty description for the colour behind the bed.

He knows what colour this room is. He's been here.

I was out of the house and into the car before I knew it. Days later, it occurred to me I should have stuffed Rebecca's hollow curtain poles with frozen shrimp. Of course, the clever moves always elude me at the time.

~ ~ ~

By the time I arrived at the Palo Alto office where James and his team were trying to create the next Silicon Valley success story, all dignity had abandoned me. I think my tears were already beginning as I lurched through the front desk area, empty because the company was too small to have a receptionist. In my haste, I then collided with the *foosball* table, which appears to be a required toy at every start-up with venture capital funding.

I spotted my husband – cropped, dark brown hair, shirt half untucked as usual – hunched over his keyboard, at the end of an untidy row of T-shirt clad computer coders. This gaggle looked barely old enough to have gained admission to Stanford University, let alone already graduated.

James looked up and noticed me. Surprise crossed his face, but was replaced with something I assumed was guilt. I could see how deep the lines in the middle of his forehead were getting these days, and how weary he looked.

'Purple,' was all I managed to utter at first. Terrific. Millions of wives over the centuries have faced this situation and all I could say was *purple*.

'Grace –' He stood and took my arm, trying to get me to sit.

I wrenched myself free. 'How did you know her bedroom is purple? How did you know?'

'Listen.' He shook his head. 'It's not what you think'.

Okay, so *purple* may not have been eloquent, but at least it was original. I saw red – as well as crimson, magenta and every shade in between.

'How could you?' I hissed. 'I know what's going on. And all the time, I've been decorating that sodding room!'

'Please,' he glanced sideways at the line of coders. 'Calm down!'

Fingers had frozen over keyboards. Curious youthful faces were turned towards us: James was a popular boss.

'You knew her bedroom is purple because you've been sleeping with her, haven't you? You've been sleeping with my client!'

'No, look, it wasn't like that.'

'No, you look. Look at this purple and tell me you've never seen it before.' I pulled the paint sample from my purse and unscrewed the lid. Dark and liquidly sinister, I waved it dangerously close to his computer.

'Okay, okay, I'm sorry. Please – calm down and let me tell you.' By now his dark brown eyes were wide with panic.

The whole office had fallen silent, but I saw that not everyone was watching us. Instead, some of them had turned to the far side of the room, as Rebecca stood and began heading our way. I realised most of them knew she had a part in this drama. And what about Rebecca? Was she half expecting this to happen? There I was, a total mess inside and out, and she appeared to be perfectly composed.

She came closer and I caught the eye contact between her and James. He had now turned paler than I'd ever seen, including the time he got food poisoning in Turkey and couldn't stand for three days. As she walked behind the desks of her co-workers, most of them didn't seem to know whether to freeze or flee.

'Look,' she said, 'let's not do this here.' Not a blonde hair was out of place.

'Where would you rather *do it*?' I snapped back, but my voice was quivering. 'Your bedroom? With my husband?'

James reached for me again, but seemed to change his mind and let his hand drop. 'I know you're furious right now, but it was just one stupid mistake in Vegas,' he said quietly.

'I don't believe you! You've been in her bedroom!' I was looking wildly from one to the other, sick with the thought of them wrapped around each other.

'Well, actually,' Rebecca had the nerve to put her hand on his arm, 'it's probably best that you know, Grace. It wasn't a mistake.' She glanced at me and I noticed for the first time an intense determination in her face. 'I'm so sorry, we didn't plan it this way. It happened after I hired you. But we can't help how we feel.' In her strappy beige sandals she was nearly as tall as James, and she barely needed to lift her pointy little chin upwards to gaze at my husband adoringly. 'The thing is, I care about you and I want to be with you.'

A collective gasp flew round the office, almost loud enough to drown my yelp of pain. I could sense the techie crowd reaching for their phones to post *Wild and crazy work love triangle* on their Facebook pages. I felt like I'd been whacked in the ribs with a cricket bat, but I registered through my tears that James was shaking his head in defeat. The little pot slipped from my fingers before I could think of throwing paint in their faces. Instead, it added a permanent souvenir of the demise of my marriage to the carpet and his Hush Puppies. Rebecca sidestepped smartly and her sexy sandals escaped the shower. Too bad.

Failing entirely to live up to my name, I turned and fled with as much poise as a double-decker London bus.

~ ~ ~

We spent the next two days in an ugly blur of sobbing, shouting, and silence. Not all the tears were mine: James followed me straight home and begged me to hear his side of the story. I heard but I didn't listen and I certainly didn't believe his lame attempts to blame his cheating on a drunken night of clubbing at the conference in Las Vegas. Did he really think I was that gullible?

He tiptoed around me for the first evening, then slept in our guest room and left early the next day. That was worse than the awkwardness of him being in the apartment: I knew he was going to see Rebecca and I was tormented by the thought. I wasn't even sure he'd come home again. But he did, to find me curled up on the sofa with a blanket, in pointed denial of the California sunshine outside.

'Will you please talk to me?' He approached hesitantly. 'I know this was really, really stupid but I need to tell you my side of things.'

'You mean you've got something original to say? Because up to this point, it's all looking like one big cliché to me. You cheated, you got caught, you're a lying bastard.'

He sat down at the other end of our Ikea sofa and I immediately tucked my legs under me, as if it would burn me to touch him. 'Grace, I didn't lie to you, I was trying to tell you!'

'Well, you didn't try very hard.' I could feel my eyes welling up yet again.

'Look, ever since I got back, I've been trying to get you to sit down.' He did at least have the decency to look distraught. 'But you've been so caught up in your business recently – there wasn't a good moment.'

He was staring at me intently and I could see the beginning of tears in his own eyes. He clearly hadn't shaved that morning and his shirt was even more of a crumpled disaster than usual.

'Well, excuse me for turning my back for five minutes to try and make some money.' I was firmly on the defensive, one hundred per cent the injured party. 'And in case you hadn't noticed, I was slaving away to finish a project for the woman you're sleeping with!'

'I'm not sleeping with her. It was just one time. One stupid bloody time. I'm so sorry.'

'I don't believe you. You knew about that goddamn purple wall.' I was looking around wildly, seeking my escape route. I didn't want to be in the same room with him.

'All right, so I happened to see her bedroom! That doesn't mean anything.'

'No, it means everything.' I was sobbing now. 'It means I'll never trust you again.'

I wish I'd had the panache to storm out of our apartment in an expensive cloud of Chanel perfume. I wish I'd owned a Louis Vuitton bag to grab on my way to check into a luxury hotel, where I'd instigate a passionate revenge fling with a nineteen-year-old bellboy. Unfortunately, I clambered off the sofa with pins and needles in my legs and tripped over my blankie instead. Then I trailed soggy tissues across the floor and locked myself in the bathroom, where my only company was a dog-eared copy of *National Geographic*.

I had followed my British husband – and his job – from London to California, but my own attempt at the American dream had flopped. I'd been working crazily, had failed to see my marriage falling apart, and felt like a total fool.

I certainly couldn't afford to kick James out and stay in our apartment on my own. My so-called business was barely breathing. I had no idea how many months or years of scraping by might be ahead of me, if I attempted to build a list of design clients who weren't going to thank me by stealing my husband. Did I have the energy to move out, find a job, and rebuild my life in the fast-moving world of Silicon Valley? What the heck was I doing in this country, anyway? All I wanted was to crawl under the bed covers and hide, preferably with a packet of imported Cadbury's biscuits.

In the small, mocking hours of the next morning, I found myself unearthing a suitcase from the closet. With safety, seclusion and comfort food as my primary motives, I booked a flight home to England.

~~~

Author's note: *Saving Saffron Sweeting* is a full-length book, and was a quarter-finalist in the Amazon Breakthrough Novel Award. To continue reading, please visit:
http://mybook.to/sweeting

From the Author

Independent authors like me rely on reviews from readers to help spread the word about our work. Please consider adding your review of *Attention Span and other stories* to Amazon, Goodreads and other online forums.

If you enjoyed these stories, you may also like *Saving Saffron Sweeting* and two further novels set in the same English village. You can learn more and purchase it at: http://mybook.to/sweeting

I love to connect with readers through my website and social media. Visit www.paulinewiles.com for news, bonus materials and special promotions. You can also sign up for my newsletter to be notified of new releases and receive two free bonus guides: *50 British Foods to Try Before You Die* and *60 Things to Know Before Your First Trip to England*.